His attraction to Rina made no sense, he knew. Maybe attraction never made sense. It had happened to him before, seeing a girl and feeling something click inside him. But a *vampire*?

Rina was so close beside him that when he breathed, he inhaled her faint scent, but he was half afraid to look at her. His fingers brushed his throat uneasily. He remembered the sharp nip he had felt there when she had crept into his room. . . .

James sneaked a glimpse at her. Her beauty always shocked him—the odd amber eyes, the wild raven hair. It was as if he kept forgetting what she looked like. Maybe that was because when he thought of her, it wasn't as a picture in his head but more as a scent or a touch. . . . It was impossible, he told himself, that he could be falling for a vampire. . . .

Don't miss the beginning of this
exciting miniseries:

Volume I: *Blood Curse*

VAMPIRE'S LOVE

VOLUME TWO

BLOOD SPELL

BY

JANICE HARRELL

SCHOLASTIC INC.
New York Toronto London Auckland Sydney

ISBN 0-590-60390-6

Produced by Daniel Weiss Associates, Inc.
33 West 17th Street, New York, NY 10011

12 11 10 9 8 7 6 5 4 3 2 1   5 6 7 8 9/9 0/0

First Scholastic printing, November 1995

1

Molly Haggerty and Laura Blalock sat in a dark booth at Pizzeria Speciale, munching on pizza. A Ouija board lay on the table between them, its planchette askew. "I dunno," said Molly. "It just doesn't want to speak to me tonight. I don't call *mmph* a message, do you?"

A jukebox blared a country-and-western tune, and a waitress brushed by their table carrying a tray of drinks. "Maybe the board doesn't like the atmosphere here," said Laura. "There's an awful lot of noise."

"Well, I can't take it home. My parents would have a fit."

"They're still mad, huh?"

"I'll say. My dad keeps saying the house got 'trashed' during my séance. Okay, maybe a couple of things got broken—people *did* sort of panic when Chelsea's spirit spoke—but I certainly wouldn't say it was trashed, would you?"

"No, just that one broken lamp and a few

other things. And it was a *great* séance! Chelsea sounded so real—like she was actually in the room."

"Poor James. He and Chelsea were the perfect couple. Who would have ever dreamed that something like this would happen? It's just awful." Molly blew her nose noisily.

"We don't know what happened," Laura pointed out. "We don't even know for sure that Chelsea's dead. It's not like there was a body or even any witnesses." She fished a newspaper clipping from her purse and smoothed it out on the table. "Did you see this?"

TEEN STILL MISSING

Police have no leads in the disappearance of Chelsea Hammond, 17, of Tyler Falls. Hammond was last seen on September 23 when she and a classmate attended a movie at Golden Leaf Mall. Her classmate reported she left the mall at about ten o'clock when the movie ended. Hammond never reached home. She was driving a 1989 white Mazda and is believed to be wearing an olive-green sweater and a short, flowered skirt. Police are asking anyone who has any information on her whereabouts to call Crime Stoppers. Crime Stoppers wants your information, not your name.

Molly peered at it. "It's not a very big story, is it?"

"I've noticed the newspaper write-ups are getting smaller and smaller," said Laura.

"Maybe that means the police are giving up," Molly said.

"I don't think so. It just means they don't have any leads, like they say."

"If only we knew what happened to her!" cried Molly. "But to have her vanish like that without a trace . . ."

"It's weird that she was with that new girl, Rina Cargiale, that night. I mean, when you think about it, Rina was actually the last person to see Chelsea alive."

"Are you suggesting . . ." Molly stared at her friend wide-eyed.

"Nah," said Laura hastily. "The whole idea is ridiculous. I don't know why I even said it." She lowered her voice. "I guess what made me think of that is I saw Rina standing with James in front of the lockers yesterday and—I don't know how to explain it—there was a kind of electricity in the air. It was weird."

"I've seen them together," said Molly. She twisted her napkin into a tight corkscrew and glanced anxiously at Laura. "Do you think Rina and James have something going? Are you thinking that would give Rina a *motive*?"

Laura frowned. "Nah. When you say it out loud, I hear how crazy it sounds. Nobody murders somebody just to get a boyfriend."

"I thought he was still heartbroken about poor Chelsea," said Molly uncomfortably.

"Yeah." Laura looked down. "But I think he must really like Rina. You should have seen them together."

"But do you think he suspects that Rina—" Molly broke off and her eyes narrowed. "The girl *is* strange, Laura. The way she looks at you without blinking, even. And her eyes are such a funny color."

"Contact lenses," said Laura. "She's probably got new ones. It took me ages to learn to blink after I got them."

"I don't know—there's something about her. . . ." Molly clenched her fists. "When I ran into James in the hall the other day, he looked right through me. Half the time he hardly seems to know what he's doing. I thought it was because of Chelsea, but *what if he knows that Rina killed her!*"

Laura squirmed uncomfortably. "It's not like we have any evidence. We can't go around accusing people of murder right and left. I don't know what's happening to me. I'm going completely paranoid."

Molly shivered. "I know. All of us are scared. My parents didn't even want me to come out tonight. I had to promise I'd park right out front, under the lights."

"I just don't know what to think."

Molly pounded on the Ouija board. "Why won't you speak to us, stupid?"

"Let's try it again," suggested Laura.

"It's not going to work," said Molly putting her fingers on the planchette. She closed her eyes. "Wait a minute! It's moving!" she cried.

"*V!*" cried Laura victoriously.

The planchette joltingly spelled out V-A-M-P-I-R-E-S.

"Look at that!" cried Molly. "It spelled out *vampires*. That's more like it. It makes more sense than *mmph*, anyway."

Laura wrinkled her nose. "Not really. Not when you think about it. There's no such thing as vampires."

Molly picked up her slice of pizza. "You're right. This is stupid." She stared out the window at the darkness of the parking lot outside. "I wonder what James is doing tonight."

"Probably thinking about poor Chelsea," said Laura.

"Poor, poor Chelsea," Molly echoed.

At Rina's house on Oak Street, hundreds of crystal prisms in the big chandelier of the dining room shivered as Chelsea walked under it, smiling menacingly at James and Rina. Her flesh was strangely bleached of color, and her eyes looked hard and shallow, like jewel chips. Her heels clicked on the parquet floor, and she leered as she stepped through the open archway into the hall. With horror James saw that she had two sharp fangs. They indented her bottom lip where they pressed against the flesh. James clutched Rina's hand more tightly, wanting to run, but at the open front door, blocking their escape, stood Trip Davis, his arms held out stiffly on either side of him. James glanced at him and shuddered. Trip seemed to fill up the big doorway, but even more frightening was he seemed unaware that his mouth was bloody.

Suddenly Rina kicked Trip and ducked under his outstretched arm. He doubled over in pain, and James made a break for it. Leaping off the front porch, he kept running, not daring to look over his shoulder. His feet sank into the grass, and he felt as if he were running in slow motion. His breath tore painfully at his throat. Rina threw open the door when he reached the car, and James slid in behind the wheel, gasping for breath. It seemed to take him an eternity to fit his keys into the ignition. He was vaguely conscious that Trip and Chelsea were yelling at him, but he gunned the motor. Their voices were drowned out when the car leaped ahead.

A few minutes later James realized the speedometer was still pushing sixty—and he was in a residential neighborhood. He forced himself to ease up on the gas pedal and made himself exhale slowly.

"We made it," he said, glancing at Rina. "We got away."

Trip stared dumbfounded at the disappearing taillights.

"You let them get away!" Chelsea shrieked.

Trip shrugged. "Big deal. I can't help it if they got away—I was standing right at the door when they opened it, just like you told me to be."

"But you were so full of blood you could hardly move—so you weren't much good, were you?" snapped Chelsea. "You just had to sneak out and have a snack, I guess."

Trip blushed. "A neighbor down the street was taking out his trash. I just took a little bit of his blood. I didn't kill him or anything."

"For this you blew our big chance!"

"Look, if you wanted to catch them so bad, nothing was stopping *you* from going after them," Trip retorted.

"Except that I ran smack into you, remember?" Chelsea had taken her time getting up after she and Trip had collided, but she didn't go into that. She wouldn't like to admit she had been afraid to run after Rina alone. Getting James would be easy, but Rina was a vampire and dangerous.

"Oh, shut up, Chelsea." Trip went into the kitchen and splashed cold water on his mouth. The water ran pink into the stainless-steel sink. He tore some paper towels off a nearby roll and blotted his face.

Chelsea followed him into the kitchen, frowning. She hoped Trip wasn't going to be a pain. She found his beefy looks uninspiring, and she wished he'd cut the wiry hair that bushed out like unruly shrubbery below his ears. But there was one thing she did like about him: Ever since she had made him into a vampire in Molly's toolshed on the night of the séance, he had been touchingly dependent on her.

If he started giving her a hard time, she wasn't going to put up with it, she decided. The thing she liked most about being a vampire was she didn't have to put up with anything she didn't like. She didn't have to go to school, she didn't have to live at home with her parents, and she sure wasn't going to take a bunch of junk from Trip.

"That was close," said Rina. "I don't understand it. I thought Chelsea'd still be wandering around confused and wondering what happened. After all, she hasn't been a vampire very long, right?"

"Don't ask me," said James wearily. "I'm not the one who did it to her."

"It was an accident," Rina whimpered. "She must have gotten my blood in her mouth when she bit me." She regarded him with anxious eyes. "You aren't still mad at me, are you, James?"

James shook his head. "I'm past being mad, Rina. I'm numb. I don't know. . . . This is such a mess."

His attraction to Rina made no sense, he knew. Maybe attraction never made much sense. It had happened to him before, seeing a girl and feeling something click inside him. But a *vampire*?

Rina was so close beside him that when he breathed, he inhaled her faint scent, but he was half afraid to look at her. His fingers brushed his throat uneasily. He remembered the sharp nip he had felt there when she had crept into his room. He had been unhappy enough then to willingly bare his throat to Rina. He couldn't believe he had done that. Those nights he had let Rina drink his blood seemed years ago instead of only weeks. Now he realized the last thing he wanted was to end up a vampire like Chelsea and Trip. He couldn't take a chance on any more nighttime visits from Rina.

James sneaked a glimpse at her. Her beauty always shocked him—the odd amber eyes, the wild raven hair. It was as if he kept forgetting what she looked like. Maybe that was because when he thought of her, it wasn't as a picture in his head but more as a scent or a touch. Even hearing someone say her name called forth a torrent of emotions he couldn't sort out. He gripped the steering wheel tightly. It was impossible, he told himself, that he could be falling for a vampire. Even being friends with her he was taking a chance.

"Okay, what do we do next?" he demanded. "We got away from them this time, but it's not like they don't know where to find us. They're bound to try again."

Rina shivered. "Chelsea must have made herself into a mist and squeezed in. That's a very tricky thing to do. Your mind has to be completely blank."

"I'll take your word for it," said James wryly.

"She must have learned how from another

vampire." Rina glanced at him. "Somebody's been teaching her tricks."

"Wait a minute!" James stared. "Are you telling me we've got to worry about *three* vampires?"

Rina shrugged. "I don't know, but something awfully funny is going on. I think we'd better go back to the house and try to find out what's happening."

"Are you out of your mind?" James exploded. "We were lucky to get away. I'm not crazy enough to give those guys two chances at me in one night."

"They won't even see us," Rina argued. "We can park one street over and sneak through the woods to the house. We need to find out what they're up to, don't we?"

James caught a glimpse of himself in the rearview mirror. In the dim light he could see the gleam of his fair hair. He could feel his heart beating and feel his jeans pressing against his thighs. If it hadn't been for such tangible evidence, he would have almost thought he was dreaming. How could this be happening to him?

It had occurred to him that he could escape the whole mess by running away to his grandmother's place in the mountains. The plan had made sense. But now that it came down to it, he couldn't bring himself to leave Rina. And obviously there was no way he could show up at his grandmother's with her in tow. Explain Rina to his grandmother? He couldn't even explain her to himself.

"Turn here," said Rina. "Then we'll double back on Elm Street."

James didn't have a better idea, so he gritted his teeth and turned the car around.

"Can you believe this? Rina doesn't have a microwave," complained Chelsea, glancing around the kitchen. "There's nothing at all around here that we can sell for cash. No TV, no VCR. Just a bunch of stuff nobody wants, like china and lace doilies."

"What do you have in mind, Chels? Gonna have a garage sale?"

"All I want," she said, "is to make James into a vampire so we can all be together again—all three of us buddies together, you, me, and him. Any loot I can grab is purely extra." She frowned. "Hmm, if a bunch of witches is a coven, I wonder what you call it when it's vampires?"

Trip put his arm around her and squeezed tight. "A clutch," he growled.

Chelsea pushed him away. "Cut it out, Trip."

He frowned unhappily. "James is still it for you, isn't he? What's so great about him? He's not a vampire, and he doesn't want to be one, either."

"Yes, but once we *make* him into a vampire, then he'll like it. Don't worry—we didn't get him tonight, but we'll have another chance."

"I don't know how you figure that." Trip's frown deepened. "We scared him silly tonight. I've never seen him run so fast, not even at a track meet."

Chelsea shrugged. "Okay, he was scared, but

he'll calm down. Pretty soon he'll start telling himself he was imagining things. It's kind of hard to believe that vampires are after you, right? Next thing you know James will be thinking he overreacted."

"But what about Rina?" asked Trip. "*She's* not going to think she overreacted. She knows vampires are real because she's one herself."

"Oh, we can handle Rina," she said blithely. "There are two of us, and we're bigger than she is."

"I think we ought to give up on James," said Trip.

Chelsea stamped her foot. "I'll never give up. Nobody can stay scared twenty-four hours a day. We'll just act like nothing happened, and then they'll get careless and fall right into our laps." She opened the refrigerator's freezer compartment and peeked into it.

"This is a pretty strange time to go looking for ice cubes," Trip said irritably.

"I'm checking for cash," explained Chelsea. "The freezer is the number one place people hide money."

"You're kidding me!"

"No, seriously. I guess they're thinking 'cold cash' and the next thing you know, they're socking a roll of bills next to the ice cubes." She opened the bottom part of the fridge. "Look at this! Packs of outdated blood!" She wrinkled her nose in distaste.

"Rina must have some kind of pull at the blood bank."

"Disgusting. It's not even whole blood. It's plasma."

"Blood lite!" Trip grinned. He peered over her shoulder at the labeled plastic bags stacked on the top shelf of the fridge. "This is a pretty good deal, you know? All that blood has been tested."

"You're a vampire, remember? Quit worrying about viruses." Chelsea glanced around the bare kitchen. "Let's try upstairs. Maybe she stashed something under the mattress."

"Where did you find this stuff out about where people hide money, anyway?"

"From a vampire friend." Chelsea grinned. "Isn't it funny how in school they never teach you anything you really need to know?"

The two vampires bounded lightly upstairs. "I feel like I'm floating!" exclaimed Trip. "It's like being on a trampoline."

"Easiest way in the world to lose a hundred pounds is to turn into a vampire," said Chelsea. "It only works after dark, of course. When the sun comes up every morning, I feel like I weigh a ton."

She opened a door at the end of the upstairs hall. The room was as bare of personal touches as a hotel room. Only a pair of jeans draped over the back of a chair told her that it belonged to Rina.

A shadow moved across the window. Chelsea grabbed Trip's arm. "What's that?" she cried.

"Just a bird," said Trip.

"Birds don't fly at night." Chelsea dashed over to the window, leaned on the sill and peered anxiously into the darkness.

"I don't know what you're so worked up

about," said Trip. "James and Rina must be miles away by now."

Chelsea couldn't explain why she was uneasy, because she had never told Trip that vampires could change into bats. Her theory was if he started learning vampire tricks, it would be harder to control him. That was why she had decided to keep her new skills to herself. She gave a little laugh. "I guess I'm a bundle of nerves," she said. "It'll do me good to get home. A little boring routine is just what I need right now."

"If you go home," Trip warned her, "you're going to have a whole lot of explaining to do. In case you didn't know it, cops all over the Southeast are looking for you. Everybody and his brother thinks you've been kidnapped. Now all of a sudden you decide to show up? It means you're going to have to tell your parents what happened, that's all."

"Not a chance. You should see the way they act when I come in ten minutes after curfew. I can just *imagine* how they'd freak out if I told them I'm one of the undead."

"The cops are going to ask you a lot of questions," Trip continued.

"I know how to handle them." Chelsea smirked. "I've decided I'm going to be a victim of amnesia. Cool, huh? I saw somebody with amnesia on a soap once, and it worked great. My mind is, like, blank for the crucial period, see? So I won't be able to answer any questions."

"The cops—" Trip began.

"Especially not from the cops," said Chelsea firmly. She lifted the mattress. No money, but her eyes narrowed when she glimpsed something that looked like a suitcase hiding under the bed. "Whoa!" she cried. She got down on her hands and knees and peered under the bed. "Look at this!" She pulled out an ancient leather bag. "The leather's falling apart." She opened it. "If I were Rina, I would pitch this old thing and get something better, alligator hide, maybe." Chelsea pulled a yellowed ivory cameo choker out of the bag and wound its black ribbon around her hand. She peered at the miniature portrait that had been painted on the back of the cameo, a picture of somebody who'd been dead for hundreds of years. Who cared? She tossed it aside, then thrust probing fingers into the bag's torn lining. "Hey, this is more like it." She pulled out a ruby bracelet. Delicate gold links held one stone to another and made the bracelet as supple as a fine gold chain.

"You think those rubies are real?" asked Trip, his eyes bugging.

"Sure!" said Chelsea. "Nobody'd bother with all this fancy gold work if they were fake. Pretty, huh? And my favorite color: blood-red." She smiled as she moved her wrist a little to make the stones glimmer. The jewels glowed as if a flame moved in their depths.

"No, you don't," Trip said. "Why should you keep it all to yourself? We go halvsies on the rubies." He groped in his pocket and pulled out a packet of cigarettes, then plopped down on the bed. "Don't get all greedy, Chels. I'll bet I could buy a Corvette with what those rubies would bring."

"I don't want a Corvette. I want the rubies." Chelsea shot a hostile glance in his direction. "I thought you gave up smoking."

"Yeah, I did." He grinned. "But now that I'm a vampire I never run out of breath, and I don't have to worry about cancer, so I figured, why not?"

Chelsea's eyes shimmered as she stared at him fixedly. "Don't light it, Trip. I'm warning you!"

"James used to tell me you were bossy," he said. "Now I see just what he was talking about. Let's get one thing straight, Chels. You may have made me into a vampire, but you aren't going to lead me around by the nose. My mind was a little messed up at first—being a vampire took some getting used to. But now you can stop pushing me around. Let's remember which one of us is biggest." He grinned. "As long as we're clear about that, you and me'll get along fine." He stuck a cigarette in the corner of his mouth, then flicked the flint of his lighter. The flame lit his face with an orange glow. "For starters, hand over those rubies."

"Maybe you'd like to smoke your cigarette first," said Chelsea. She clutched the old leather bag tightly to her chest and watched as Trip lit the cigarette and sucked deeply, waiting until a red ash formed at its end.

Suddenly, Chelsea threw the leather bag in Trip's face. He swore. The cigarette fell on his shirt, and a black hole burned into the fabric. He swatted the curling plume of smoke with his hand, but when his hand touched the smoldering shirt, flames leaped from his fingers.

"Help!" he screamed.

His chest was aflame now, and fire was climbing up his flailing arms. As if he had been doused in gasoline, the flames flared suddenly and engulfed him. He threw himself to the floor and rolled desperately around on the rug. Chelsea heard the crackling of the fire as Trip kicked and writhed on the braided rug. His body was already black in the heart of the spinning flames. In minutes he was no more than a silent stick figure.

Chelsea stepped back, pressing herself against the wall, her eyes wide in horror.

Then the fire sputtered out, and all that remained of Trip was a scorched pattern, a jagged oblong of ash, still smoldering on the braided rug. Chelsea was afraid to stamp on the burning fibers to put them out.

A faint haze of smoke hung in the room and stung her nostrils. She shivered uncontrollably. "I warned him," she whispered. "I told him not to light it, and he did it anyway. It was his own fault!"

2

Clinging to the eaves above the open window of the bedroom, a bat hung upside down. Its ears, dwarfing its ugly face, were pink folds of flesh with bristles of sensitive hair to catch every vibration in the air. A swarm of gnats rattled the air nearby, but even that intriguing insect sound could not distract the bat from the tense voices of the two vampires talking inside the house. When the bat heard the crackle of flames, it released its grasp on the eaves at once and soared past the window. The bat's furry body was so light that with its wings outstretched, it floated. It bobbed a moment on the warm currents of air that blew out the window, then moved its wings in a resolute swimming motion and flew toward the nearby woods. Its eyes were tiny golden dots above its fleshy snout, and when it opened its mouth, it showed jagged fangs. "Rina," it sighed. The bat deftly alit, hanging by its claws from a tree branch.

It had perched in a thin stand of trees that

encircled the house's broad lawn. The woods were a mixture of pines and hardwoods, where the bat could hear the click of beetles and the scurrying sound of a field mouse making its way under some matted pine straw. Pale moonlight worked its way through the tree canopy in spots, but the bat was conscious only of a world of vibrations where the air shuddered with every movement.

Gripping the rough bark with its claws, the small creature scurried claw over claw along the branch and then began backing down the tree trunk, feeling its way. At last it fell with a faint rustle onto the dry leaves that covered the ground. It moved haltingly over the leaf matter, pulling itself along with a clumsy movement of its clawed wings. As it limped along, the little creature swelled as if it were being pumped up with air. The long thin bones of its wings grew coarse and thick, and the loose skin that hung between the wing bones shrank. Then the air around it shuddered as it exploded into a huge, black furry creature that in the uncertain moonlight looked like a Saint Bernard. Except for its huge, strangely fleshy ears and its grotesque, snub-nosed face—the face of a vampire bat.

The buzz and click of the insects in the woods went silent suddenly as if the natural world were startled by the strange metamorphosis. The monster standing among the trees continued to change. Its vertebrae stretched as it grew taller and thinner. Its fur became sparse; then suddenly the skin was naked and blanching to ivory. At last the strange creature straightened up and shook its hair. A shard of moonlight filtering through the trees revealed it was wearing jeans and a light-colored shirt. "Rina!" she said resolutely, remembering her name. She ran her hands up her sides to reassure herself she was once again in her human shape.

James heard a movement and spun around. "Rina?" he whispered anxiously. "Is that you?"

Rina smoothed her black hair as she stepped out of the shadows into the clearing where he stood. "I wish you wouldn't stare like that," she complained. "When I've been changing, I get self-conscious."

"I couldn't see where you had gone to," he said. "I was worried." He eyed her uneasily. "What's so embarrassing? I thought you were just going to sneak up close to the house and listen."

Her face darkened with a blush. "I changed into a bat," she confessed.

James gulped. Looking at Rina now, he found himself thinking that maybe her hair was bat-colored. He shut his eyes. "Could you hear what they were saying? What did you find out?"

Rina's expression changed. "I've got bad news, James."

He grabbed her arms. "What happened? Tell me!"

"Trip is dead."

James staggered several steps backward. "But he's a vampire now!" he gasped. "Vampires can't die!"

Rina licked her lips. "Remember I told you

there are ways for us to die? Well, Chelsea set him on fire. I think they were fighting over my ruby bracelet. Chelsea wanted to wear it, and Trip wanted to sell it and buy a Corvette."

James stared at her blankly.

"I guess you haven't seen my bracelet." Rina took a deep breath. "I don't wear it anymore because I have very bad memories connected with it. The guy who gave it to me is the one who made me into a vampire. Chelsea can have the stupid thing. I don't want it. It certainly wasn't worth killing Trip over."

James was struggling to understand. "What happened, Rina?"

"Chelsea dropped a cigarette onto Trip's shirt. Well, technically, he dropped it, but she made it happen."

"And that killed him?" asked James, bewildered.

"Flames destroy vampires almost instantly. I guess Trip didn't realize."

"Rina—" James hesitated "—are you *sure* he's dead?"

Rina nodded. "I could hear his screams. I flew by and saw he was on fire, and when the fire sputtered out a minute later, I heard Chelsea say that it wasn't her fault."

"That's Chelsea, all right," said James. "Whatever happens, it's never her fault." A breeze stirred the tree branches. "Maybe Chelsea figures she can sell the rubies to make a getaway," he added. "Maybe she wants to go to South America or someplace.

She never did like North Carolina. She was always saying she hated living in a dinky little town where there's nothing to do."

Rina glanced over her shoulder at the brightly lit house, visible through the trees. "Maybe it's a lot more interesting for her, now that she's become a vampire."

James shuddered.

"I wish I could say she's leaving town," said Rina, "but she's not. I heard her say she's going to tell her parents she has amnesia. That way they can't ask her any questions about what happened while she was missing."

James ran his fingers through his hair. "You mean to tell me she's going to go back to school as if nothing happened? She hates school. You're saying that after she's become a vampire and murdered Trip, she's going to go back to taking algebra tests? Is she figuring she can lure kids over to the pencil sharpener and suck their blood?" He became uncomfortably aware that he was spouting off wildly. He hoped he hadn't said something that hurt Rina's feelings. "It's such a shock," he said apologetically. "I don't know—I keep expecting to find out it's all a mistake."

The moonlight filtering into the clearing seemed threatening, as if it were trying to steal his reason. Trip dead! It was hard to believe that a guy who had been his friend, a two-hundred-pound football tackle, had vanished in a puff of smoke. Or that Chelsea had killed him.

James took a deep breath. "What are we going to do now, Rina?"

She shrugged. "Go to school in the morning as usual. Only we'd better stick together. We don't want Chelsea to catch us by surprise."

"And that's *all*? That's the plan?"

Rina looked at him shyly. "I don't know if I've mentioned it: Vampires lose their supernatural strength when the sun comes up. They slow down and can't change shape or anything. So I don't think Chelsea will try to make a kill in broad daylight, because it's more risky. I mean, it's not like she can just turn into a vapor and float away leaving no fingerprints, the way she can at night. And in the daytime, you're stronger than she is, James. You'd have a good chance of fighting her off."

James could feel cold sweat beading on his brow.

"We'll probably be okay as long as we only see her at school," said Rina.

"Gee, that's a big comfort."

Rina shrugged again. "It's not much, but it's what we've got."

"I'd better go on home," James said. "I don't know what else to do. I just hope she isn't waiting for me when I get there." He suddenly realized he had a headache.

"It didn't sound to me as if she planned to try anything else tonight. She said she was going home, so I expect that's what she'll do." Rina glanced at him from beneath her lashes. "She may be a little shaken up after killing Trip."

"Jeez! I hope so," said James with feeling.

They walked back to his car. He started to reach for her hand, but suddenly he couldn't bear to touch her cold flesh and thrust his hands in his pockets instead. Rina's shape seemed shifting and unsteady in the moonlight. James could hear his own feet crushing the dry leaves, but Rina's steps were silent. In the moonlight she seemed more like a hallucination than a girl. It was enough to drive anybody out of their senses. Thinking about how she had turned into a bat was bad enough, but worse was the uncomfortable feeling that she had secrets she hadn't shared with him. Yet he wasn't sure he even wanted to know what her life had been like before they met.

"I can't believe this," he said. "This isn't happening!"

Rina looked embarrassed. "I know it's hard to believe, but that's sort of good, you know? A plus for me. Up till everybody got so science-minded, if vampires got caught, people would try to do awful things to them—put stakes through their hearts, set them on fire with torches. . . . But nowadays, even if somebody does find out the truth, they don't do a thing. They can't make themselves believe it. They figure they're going crazy." She smiled. "It's a piece of luck for me."

James was relieved when they got to his car, which was parked at the curb on Elm Street. Up and down the street, buttery squares of light showed in the windows of the big frame houses, and the street seemed reassuringly normal. Even Rina, under the powerful halogen streetlight, took on substance. She looked like any other girl—only more beautiful—and he felt himself thinking she wasn't a bit like Chelsea. He sensed a sweetness and purity in her that nothing in her strange life had been able to destroy.

Tonight she was wearing a blue pin-striped shirt with her jeans, but the shirt seemed quite different from the ones he wore. It was prettily tailored, gathered in tucks at the shoulder and with slightly full sleeves tapered into narrow wristbands. He had an idea she was taking more trouble with her clothes lately. But wasn't it ridiculous to say that a girl was clothes-conscious, when she had only just finished turning into a bat?

"You can't go back to that house tonight," he said abruptly. "You saw just now how easy it was for Chelsea to get in. There's no guarantee she won't come back. Where are you going to sleep tonight?"

"Oh, I'll be okay." Rina's eyes shifted.

With a sinking feeling in his stomach, James recognized the evasive look. "Rina, tell me the truth. Don't lie to me."

"I don't sleep," she admitted in a small voice.

"Never?"

She shook her head.

James groaned as he wrenched the car door open. Every time he felt, just for a little while, that he was an ordinary guy talking to an ordinary girl, a trapdoor opened under his feet. He couldn't bring himself to say good-bye to her.

As he drove off he didn't look back or check the rearview mirror. He was too scared of what he might see.

Rina stared into the darkness several minutes after the car's taillights disappeared from sight, feeling a sick ache in her heart. It was easy to see James was revolted by every small sign that she was a vampire. That had shown in his unguarded expression when she admitted she never slept.

She leaped up lightly into a nearby tree and sat on the branch, her eyes hot with pain. Her love could never accept her as she was—and the thought twisted in her like a knife.

Maybe, she thought, she could remember how to sleep if she tried hard enough. She should try to relax and breathe evenly as she had seen people do. And make her mind a blank—but not so blank that she turned into a mist and blew away. She hummed a lullaby to herself, a song her mother used to sing, and as she hummed it she closed her eyes.

But sleep would not come. She had forgotten how to do it, she realized. She clutched her knees tightly and choked on a sob. A wind sighed in the pine needles and dried the wet tear streaks on her cheeks.

3

At the Raleigh–Durham airport, Vlad Tzara found a seat near a screen that displayed the arrival and departure times of flights. A few yards away passengers were lining up to buy plane tickets, but plane tickets were the last thing on the vampire's mind. He was dark and strikingly handsome, with his hair pulled back in a ponytail and an antique jeweled earring dangling from one of his earlobes.

He took a folded envelope from his pocket and read the letter inside it for the tenth time. The letter writer seemed to have gotten him confused with his grandfather. Vlad glanced over it. "Deepest respects . . . legendary vampire . . . most ancient and evil lineage . . . your most obedient servant. . . ." The handwriting in the letter looked spidery and frail. Maybe the old magician hadn't heard that Vlad's grandfather had had a fatal encounter with a sharp wooden stake over a century ago. No problem. Vlad planned to show up on the appointed day, as the letter writer had suggested, and see what happened. He believed in taking things as they came.

It was a couple of days before he was due to meet the magician, though, and he figured he might as well spend the time tracking down Chelsea.

He opened her suitcase in his lap, not surprised to find little inside: a pair of jeans, a T-shirt, a couple of rayon skirts—only the few things Chelsea had bought for their trip to Las Vegas. Her distinctive perfume clung to her clothes, and the familiar scent made him smile. In another century Vlad might have taken off after her that moment, following her trail with his keen senses. But in recent times he had learned from bitter experience that an attempt to track someone by scent was apt to lead only to automobile exhaust and hot rubber on asphalt. The modern world required other methods.

A businessman sat down nearby and cast a curious glance at the suitcase open on Vlad's lap. "Got the wrong suitcase, son? It happened to me once, and it took two weeks for the airline to trace my bag. If you'll take my advice, you'll switch to carry-on luggage." The businessman patted the bulging bag on the floor. "I never let go of mine these days."

Vlad slammed Chelsea's suitcase closed. He was hungry, and he could feel the roof of his mouth tingling as his fangs slid out of their sheaths. But he observed, with a sudden sharp loss of appetite, that the businessman was grossly obese. Vlad hated digging his fangs through layers of fat. He wished Americans would lay off the french fries.

"It's my girlfriend's bag," he said shortly.

The businessman gave him an odd look. Probably he had noticed the Transylvanian accent. Vlad had not been able to rid himself of it, but that didn't bother him. He was convinced girls found his accent irresistible.

He smiled ruefully. He had to admit he had underestimated Chelsea. She wasn't nearly as much the dumb blond as he had thought. She had tricked him.

He had waited half an hour for her to return with the car before it occurred to him to go and check on her. As soon as he had found her parking space empty, he knew she was gone. Having him get the luggage had only been a ploy to get him out of the way while she left the airport without him.

It was annoying to be discarded so casually when he had taught her everything she knew about being a vampire. She would have been helpless without him—though it was true she had a certain basic aptitude for the life. He had never seen anybody pick up so quickly the knack of turning into mist. He even felt a grudging admiration for her cleverness in tricking him. She would be surprised to see him when he showed up, but she would respect him for tracking her down.

They had had fun together once and could again, he figured.

He stood up, abandoning Chelsea's luggage without a thought. Airport security would dynamite the unattended bag, no doubt. Lifting his own slender suitcase, he moved toward the door. He was pleased to note that the glass doors swung open at once in obedience to his will.

Setting off, he followed signs that said AIRPORT EXIT. As he walked, he fished Chelsea's driver's license from his pocket and gazed at it with satisfaction. A stamp-sized picture in the license's right-hand corner showed a broad-jawed blond with a tiny nose. Vlad wondered if she had realized yet that her license was missing. He tucked it back in his pocket and congratulated himself for having had the foresight to steal it from her purse while she was busy playing the slot machines in Vegas. He had kept careful tabs on his girlfriends ever since Larina had taken off. Rina had disappeared from a ferry during a storm. He had been miserably seasick at the time—he had a problem with motion sickness—and when he had realized she was gone, he naturally assumed she had fallen overboard. Running water robbed a vampire of supernatural strength, so she would have been helpless in the grip of the sea. He had even shed a tear or two. It was too bad. She was very pretty, a sweet innocent type, and he had liked having her around. He had especially liked the way he could feel the envious eyes of other guys whenever she was with him. He had managed to keep her at his side for a long time with a reliable mix of magic and old-fashioned intimidation, and he had been genuinely sorry to lose her. But when he discovered that her leather bag was missing from her cabin, his grief had turned to rage. She had deliberately tricked him! All that business of pretending she was afraid of the water when she had been able to swim! Because the only explanation for the missing bag was that she had dived overboard deliberately.

Since then he had never quite trusted any of his girlfriends. He had learned from bitter experience that girls could be just as tricky and deceitful as he was.

Cars drove past him, and he coughed black exhaust out of his lungs. He hated everything about the modern world, but even a vampire could not hold back the hand of time.

He stepped boldly out onto Airport Road. He was beyond the airport's strong lights now, standing in comparative darkness. Traffic whizzed by him dangerously fast, whipping his hair loose from its rubber band and peppering him with gritty clay dust. Sawhorses and orange traffic cones littered the shoulder of the road, and heavy earth-moving equipment gleamed ominously nearby like mechanical dinosaurs. His mouth twisted. The modern world. *Bleh!*

Standing by the sign that pointed to the main highway, Vlad smiled at the headlights that zipped past him, and he stuck out his thumb.

*   *   *

When James got home, the strains of Pachelbel's *Canon* greeted him. He smiled. It was the first time he could remember since his sister had died that he found his parents listening to music. A card game was laid out on the table, and it looked as if his father was winning.

His mother glanced up at him. "Hi, sweetheart." Her fair hair was short and feathered softly against her cheeks. She had a straight, high-bridged nose, and dark lashes and eyebrows. People said James looked like her, but he had never been able to see the resemblance himself. "I must have missed you after school," she said. "I was off grocery shopping. Been out with your friends?"

"Yeah," he mumbled. It was impossible to explain that poor Trip was dead. James felt sick at the thought of it. "Guess I'd better get down to doing my homework," he choked. "I've got a lot of catching up to do." If he and Rina were going to go to school as if nothing had happened, it meant he actually had to go upstairs and read three chapters in his history book.

"Have you had anything to eat yet?" asked his mom.

Food. James had forgotten about food. "I'll make myself a sandwich."

"Gotcha," his dad said, laying down a card.

James winced.

As he moved toward the kitchen, bursts of canned laughter met him. His kid brother, Danny, was watching a sitcom in the den. James took a few cheese slices from the fridge and slapped them between two slices of bread.

He galloped upstairs, gulping down the sandwich as he went. His insides were churning, but he finished the sandwich anyway—a guy had to eat. Then he went into the upstairs bathroom and carefully probed around the sink's drainpipe with his fingers. It was just as he remembered: The pipe had a tight copper collar; no gap at all between the pipe and the wall. A few years ago his family had had a problem with mice. His mother was too tenderhearted to set traps and poison all over the house, so she had all the openings in the house plugged with copper to keep the mice out. He never thought he'd be grateful to those mice.

James went into his room and checked to make sure the window was locked. Then he drew the curtain closed. He glanced at the stack of books on his desk, vaguely aware that he had been getting further and further behind with his schoolwork. He sat down and opened his history book.

He soon finished the chapter, but he had not the remotest idea what it was about. He glanced down at the sheet of paper under his right hand and saw he had been unconsciously doodling a lively sketch of a helmeted football player. Trip. But with fangs. His snarling face was haloed with a circling swarm of bats, and the one nearest him had Chelsea's face.

James covered his own face with his hands. How could Trip be gone? Tears filled his eyes, and he tore up the sheet of paper and dropped it in his wastebasket. He forced himself to read aloud the review questions at the end of the chapter.

"Okay," he said wearily, "what's the main idea here?" It was something about manifest destiny, that was all he was clear on. Destiny. Destiny couldn't be escaped. Maybe because the seeds of it were inside a person. His own despair about his sister's death had opened a door in his life to vampires. What he didn't know was whether it was too late now to close the door.

James slammed his book shut. He refused to believe that his situation was hopeless. In spite of everything, a tiny flame of hope burned inside him. He took a shower, pulled on pajamas, climbed into bed, and fell into a troubled sleep.

4

The next morning, Chelsea's car pulled into the school parking lot, and she leaped out at once. She could hardly wait to see James. Her fangs began sliding out of their sheaths at the thought of him, and she gulped self-consciously. She had spent a lot of time on her hair and her clothes this morning. Having her fangs show would definitely ruin the effect she was after. She forced herself not to think about James, making herself envision cold, snowy mountains in a vast arctic wasteland until her fangs slid back in their sheaths. Hunger or anger could make them show at just the most awkward time.

Suddenly kids were crowding around her.

"Chelsea! It's so great to see you!" Molly Haggerty embraced her. "I nearly passed out when I got that call from you last night. I mean, my mom said I turned white as a sheet when I heard your voice. We all thought you were dead! You can't imagine what a relief it is to have you

back safe and sound. . . ." Molly's voice trailed off
uncertainly as she looked into her friend's eyes.

Chelsea gulped. She *was* dead, of course, in a
manner of speaking. But she didn't see why that
had to interfere with her social life. "It's great to be
back," she said. She quickly put on sunglasses. "It
seems so strange—to have ten days drop out of
your life like that. I guess I'm still a little unsure of
myself, you know what I mean?"

Her performance was pretty good, if she did
say so herself. Lucky thing she had been out of
school with the flu when a character in *Abiding
Light* had had amnesia. Chelsea just hoped nobody
else at school had seen that episode. She was sort
of counting on using some of the character's lines.

Laura Blalock touched Chelsea's shoulder tenta-
tively, as if to assure herself that she was real, then
shivered and glanced at the dark sky overhead. "I
think we're getting some real fall weather already."

Chelsea realized she needed to feed to warm
herself. She found herself staring in fascination at
the pulse that flickered under the skin at Laura's
throat. Her fangs stirred.

Kids were pressing forward to get a look at
Chelsea. A crowd was growing. "Great to have you
back, Chels." Confused voices swelled around her.
"You really don't remember anything?" someone
yelled.

"I suppose I must have been carjacked or something." Chelsea pressed her fingers to her temples.
"Maybe I got a concussion during the attack. But

I'm only guessing. Really, it's all a blank." She registered a bewildered expression.

The voices around her babbled on.

"Weird."

"You think Mrs. R.'s going to give you an extension on your essay?"

"Come on! That's the last thing on her mind right now!"

"Are you sure you're up to coming back to school? Maybe you've come back too soon. You don't want to push yourself and have a relapse."

"You are all so sweet," she murmured, looking around vaguely. "I'm kind of confused right now, but I guess things will work themselves out. I just want to say it's at times like this that you find out who your true friends are." She smiled and blew her classmates a kiss.

When James got to school, a crowd of kids met him at the entrance of the main building. Molly was bouncing excitedly. "Have you talked to Chelsea?" she squeaked. "She's here! She's back!"

James shook his head. Hearing Chelsea's name made him feel like a boxer who has suffered a knockout blow. Somehow, to his surprise, he remained upright.

Molly shot him a sly look from under her lashes. "Chelsea didn't call you up last night? I would have thought you'd be the first one she'd want to talk to. She called me, but we couldn't really talk because her parents kept telling her to get off the phone.

Maybe you haven't heard she's got amnesia!"

"Weird!" someone breathed.

"She has no idea what happened to her since she disappeared!" exclaimed Molly. "Can you imagine? It must be so strange to lose your memory like that. She said she suddenly realized she was driving her car down Main Street, but she had no idea how she got there! The whole time she was gone is just a blank!"

"I thought amnesia only happened on the soaps," Tom Schwartzkoff put in.

Molly shook her head. "Chelsea told me her doctor said it happens to people sometimes when they are really stressed."

"But if that were true, we'd *all* have amnesia when our research papers were due," bleated a short girl named Elizabeth.

"Chelsea could have had worse stress than a research paper." Molly lowered her voice. "Who knows what happened after she was kidnapped? She could have witnessed a murder or been in satanic rituals."

"Maybe they forced her to stab somebody in the heart. I hear that's very big in satanic rituals," Elizabeth suggested.

"Oh, cut it out, Elizabeth," Tom snapped. "Quit being such a ghoul. Where do you get these nutty ideas?"

"Well, if she'd committed murder, it would give her a good reason to lose her memory, wouldn't it?" argued Elizabeth.

. James could feel hysterical laughter bubbling inside him, threatening to burst out. Chelsea had committed murder, all right, but no one would ever find out about it. A lump formed in his throat when he thought about Trip, and it was hard for him to concentrate on what was being said around him.

"What I don't understand is how she spoke at my séance if she wasn't dead," said Molly.

"Mass hysteria," Elizabeth suggested. "You guys only *thought* you heard her voice, see? You didn't really."

"That's a bunch of junk," said Tom. "I was there, and I heard her clear as a bell. You gonna tell me I was imagining it?"

"I know! I've got it!" Molly said. "Maybe while Chelsea was out of her mind, her spirit sort of detached itself from her body and came to my séance."

"What I think is that Chelsea came to your house—the real live Chelsea, not her spirit—and she walked in the door, said something, and then laughed herself silly when we all started falling all over things in the dark," said Tom.

"But why would she want to pretend to be her own ghost?" protested Molly.

"Perverted sense of humor," Tom guessed. "She says herself she doesn't know what she was doing while she was missing. Who's to say that isn't what happened? It was pitch-black dark in the den. None of us could see a thing."

"But if she'd somehow gotten free of her

kidnappers," Molly argued, "why didn't she go home to her folks first? That's what I would have done, wouldn't you?"

"Who says she was kidnapped?" put in Tom. "She doesn't know what happened. Maybe she just snapped, went crazy. Actually, when I think about it, that would explain a lot."

"It doesn't explain anything," Molly complained irritably. "Chelsea's not the type to crack up. I've never even seen her get nervous. It seems to me that now that she's back, everything is more mysterious than ever."

"What do you think, James?" asked Elizabeth.

James shook his head numbly. "I don't know. I guess I'm in shock." He had the feeling the others expected him to leap in and defend Chelsea against all their wild accusations of murder and satanic rituals, but he just didn't have it in him. He had to keep his mouth clamped shut to stop himself from blurting out the truth.

"You must be so relieved that she's back safe," said Molly, laying a sympathetic hand on his shoulder.

They were all looking at him now. "Yeah," he said uncomfortably. "I'm real relieved."

"Poor Chelsea . . ." Molly began, but James tuned her out. It was tough for him to stand there listening to her go on about "poor Chelsea" when he knew very well that Chelsea had killed Trip and she wanted to kill him next.

"I've got to go by my locker," he muttered, detaching himself from the group.

He felt the others' gazes fasten on him as he left, and he grew warm with embarrassment. They would probably tell each other now that he was acting weird. He guessed he shouldn't have been in such a hurry to get away. Didn't they say there was safety in numbers?

He couldn't imagine how he was going to handle it when he ran into Chelsea. What if she tried to pretend nothing had changed between them? With a shudder, he remembered how she used to stand with her arm around him, so close that her warm breath tickled his neck. Now the thought of letting her get that close gave him the creeps.

He jerked open the glass front door of the main building. The sunlight that streamed in the adjacent big glass panels flooded the front hall with glare and made it look unexpectedly shabby. The unforgiving light showed a few wisps of spiderweb clinging to high corners and made the asphalt-tile floor look worn and dusty.

Suddenly James saw Chelsea turn the corner and come toward him. She smiled, and he felt the blood drain from his head. His hands were clammy, and his heart was racing.

He was surprised to see that nothing about her looked especially strange. She was pale, but except for that she looked pretty much the same as usual. Only her shimmeringly pale eyes reminded James that she was horribly changed.

A bunch of kids suddenly opened the glass door and came into the hall chattering. Arty types. One guy had on baggy pants and sandals with turquoise-colored socks. Another had long dirty locks and a strawberry-blond goatee. A couple of girls wore matching floor-length gauze skirts together with olive-green sweatshirts.

"James!" Chelsea smiled falsely and held out her arms to him.

James backed off, swallowing hard. He was morbidly conscious that the eyes of the other kids were fixed upon him. He had half expected them to move on and leave him and Chelsea alone, but none of them seemed in any hurry to go anywhere. That was fine with him. The last thing he wanted was to be alone with her.

"You've got amnesia, I hear," he said hoarsely. He stared at Chelsea's hard and shimmering eyes in amazement. For the life of him he couldn't remember what their original color had been.

She whipped a pair of sunglasses out of her purse and tucked the earpieces into her blond hair. "My folks are going to take me in to see a psychologist at lunchtime," she said. "I guess they want to get to the bottom of this amnesia thing, try to find out what's causing it." She smiled sweetly. "I tried to get in touch with you last night. I'm really sorry I missed you!"

James was so angry, he felt blood vessels expanding in his head. "Well, I'm not sorry," he said thickly. "I don't want to see you." He was uncomfortably aware that the nearby kids' jaws dropped open in surprise. His reputation as a nice guy was taking a nosedive.

"How can you say that! How can you be so mean to me?" wailed Chelsea.

James turned abuptly and walked away. His mouth was dry, and he felt vaguely sick.

"It's Rina you're interested in, isn't it?" Chelsea shrieked. "That's why you're acting this way!"

James spun around. "Rina's not the reason, and you know it." He could feel the taunt "you vampire" forming on his lips, and he caught his breath sharply. He had to get hold of himself. If he went around blurting out stuff about vampires, men in white coats would come running after him.

"Rina's no different from me!" rasped Chelsea. "She's not a bit better than me!"

James's eyes narrowed. If Chelsea kept it up, in a minute she'd be admitting in front of all these kids that she was a vampire. "Go on, Chels," James said evenly. "Tell me about it."

Chelsea took a quick glance around, suddenly aware of the audience listening rapt with attention. "That's all I've got to say," she snapped. "You're going to be sorry you treated me like this."

The first bell exploded, and James jumped. He ran down the hall, skidding as he rounded the corner. The kids he passed were no more than a blur to him, but then he saw Rina standing outside Mrs. Kimbro's class, and he stopped short, gasping in his relief.

"Rina!" he cried. He backed her against the wall, bracing himself with one hand on the wall over her head.

"James!" She laid a hand confidingly on his chest. "You didn't have any more trouble last night, did you? With Chelsea, I mean. I was so worried. I started to come over and check on you." She reddened. "But I was afraid you wouldn't like me to. You said I shouldn't come to see you at night anymore."

"I'm okay," he said abruptly. "Listen, I just saw Chelsea. She's here. And get this, she said *she's sorry she missed me* last night." He added bitterly, "I'll bet she is!"

Rina blinked. "She's here at school? Today? I didn't expect her back so fast."

"Yes. I know. I can hardly believe it myself, but I saw her. Listen, as of now, you and me are officially going together. The two of us are going to be inseparable."

Rina gave him a tremulous smile. "Oh, James," she said. "That is so *sweet*."

"It's not for real, Rina," he said with exasperation. "It's just so Chelsea will keep her distance. You're the one who said we ought to stick together."

Rina lowered her eyes. "You're right. I forgot I said that."

James felt like the worst sort of creep using Rina this way. She had admitted she was in love with him, and for him to ask her to pretend to be his girlfriend seemed low. Cruel, even. He used to think he was a pretty nice guy, but all of a sudden he hardly recognized himself. He was using Rina to protect himself!

"I don't mind if we only pretend to be in love,"

Rina said softly. "I think it will be fun for people to think I'm your girlfriend."

"The thing is," James added, avoiding her eyes, "it's no use explaining to everybody that I'm breaking up with Chelsea because she's a vampire. They'd think I was out of my mind. But if I break up with her because I like you better, that's different. Chelsea's not going to make a fool of herself chasing me all over school when everybody knows that I've dumped her for you."

"A good idea." Rina nodded. "I like it."

"I don't," said James miserably. "Here Chelsea is back from the dead and suffering from amnesia, and I dump her. What kind of jerk does that make me?"

"But, James, she's trying to *hurt* you!"

"I know. I know." James ran his fingers rapidly through his hair. "But I never thought I'd find myself in this position."

The second bell exploded at the end of the hall, and kids at once began pushing their way through the door. James had the paranoid feeling that some of his classmates were already giving him looks. It was amazing how fast the school grapevine worked. Rumors infected Tyler Falls High School like a virus.

He made his way into the classroom and groped uncertainly for his desk. When he sat down, he let his breath out in an explosive sigh.

Kennie Grant turned around in his desk and smiled at him.

Smarmy guy, James thought.

"I hear you've dumped Chelsea," Kennie said.

James shrugged uncomfortably. "We broke up. It happens."

"Kick the girl while she's down," said Kennie. "Way to go, James."

James clenched and unclenched his fists in helpless fury.

Satisfied that he'd hit a sore spot, Kennie smirked and turned back around.

Staring at the back of Kennie's head, James found himself breathing hard. He knew he looked callous and heartless dumping Chelsea now. But he couldn't worry about that. With an intensity that astonished him, he was determined to stay alive.

5

At lunchtime, James got a candy bar from the machine and went outside. He couldn't face all the staring eyes in the cafeteria. Retreating to a quiet spot between the classroom wings, he settled down on the grass beside a drainpipe. He could feel the warmth of the brick wall against his back, and he sighed with satisfaction. He needed a break from the stress in his life, but definitely.

He had been sitting there only a minute when a chill breeze raised the hairs on the back of his neck. His eyes fell on a pair of new tennis shoes, and he slowly raised his gaze to find Rina's eyes meeting his.

"Hi," said Rina. "Can I sit down?"

James's heart lifted. It didn't make any sense, but he was glad to see her. "Sure," he said gruffly. "Have a seat."

Rina settled down beside him.

"Want a bite?" He held out the candy bar to her.

She shook her head. "No, thanks."

"Oh, right," he said wryly. "I forgot. You don't eat."

Rina's eyes filled with tears. "Can't you forget even for a minute that I'm a vampire?"

James shook his head wonderingly. "Rina, I forget it all the time. That's how I ended up in this mess."

"What mess?"

James cleared his throat. "Oh, you know. Liking you and all." He bit savagely into the chocolate and for a moment chewed it with determination.

"You like me?" asked Rina.

All of a sudden he couldn't stop himself. He reached out and brushed his fingers against her pale cheek. "Yeah." He smiled. "I like you. You know that." He grinned suddenly. "Now I've got chocolate on you."

Rina scrubbed at her cheek with the tail of her shirt.

"I wish I were human," she whispered.

James felt a jolt of pain. It struck him that being with Rina was like visiting day at prison. You could look through the bars, you could feel a tug of longing, but you could only get so close. "Yeah," he said, tossing the empty candy wrapper aside. The stupid candy bar was gone, and he was still hungry. It seemed like a symbol of something.

"Look on the bright side." He smiled crookedly. "At least Chelsea's off being tested by a psychologist right now. So that means we don't have a thing to worry about for the next hour or so." The grass between the buildings looked parched. Shreds of paper littered the ground.

"If Chelsea's not around, why are you hiding here?" asked Rina.

"I just couldn't face going in the cafeteria and having everybody point at me and say, 'There he is— the guy who dumped poor Chelsea.'" James gave a short laugh. "I don't know how I ever got mixed up with her in the first place. What a nightmare."

"It's all my fault," said Rina.

James leaned back and took a deep breath. "Yup. It is. I mean, you're the one who made Chelsea into a vampire, I know that. But I'm thinking that she was sort of the same way all along. Does that make any sense?" He glanced at Rina. "Trip used to call Chelsea the Terminator." James laughed bitterly. "Funny he should say that, since it turned out he was the one she ended up terminating."

"But he couldn't have known that."

"Nope. He only called her that because of the way she treated a girl we knew in the seventh grade." James licked the chocolate off his fingers. "Jennifer Griffith was this smart girl in our class who started making all the top grades. I guess that's what Chelsea didn't like. Anyway, Chels got all her friends to giggle at Jennifer whenever she made a hundred on a test. Jennifer freaked out and started missing things on the quizzes, but that only made them giggle more. Every time Miss Hazen called Jennifer's name it was giggle time."

Rina's face darkened. "That was mean."

James shrugged. "That was seventh grade. But it *was* mean. I mean, heck, I'm not crazy about people giggling at me even now. Look at how I'm hiding out today. I think Jennifer transferred to another school. Couldn't take it. You know, it's like I always knew Chelsea had this little mean streak. But now that she's a vampire, it's coming out in bright colors. Sort of intensified. It makes me feel stupid that I used to like her. It hits me now that she's always acted like other people didn't much matter, compared to her. She had a hard time seeing other people's point of view. And look how it turns out! Look what she did to Trip!"

"When people look good, you can fool yourself about what they're like inside," said Rina. "Like with this guy Vlad that I told you about. I loved him and I thought he loved me, but then he forced me to be a vampire. I fought him, but he was stronger." Her eyes darkened. "If he'd really loved me he wouldn't have stolen my life."

James had wondered about Rina's past, but suddenly he did not want to hear about how she had been in love with another guy. He put his arm around her thin shoulders and squeezed her tight. "Forget about the guy, Rina. He was slime."

"I can't! He's the one who made me into a vampire! I never used to think about him. I never used to bother to remember anything. But lately I've been thinking about what it was like to be alive, and it seems like the bad memories come back with the good ones." She glanced at him timidly. "Do you remember your good times with Chelsea?"

"No," said James. "I'm in too foul a mood to remember any good times. All I can see is what a mess I've made of things."

"You ought not to blame yourself."

"But that's what I'm saying, Rina," he argued. "I know it was your fault for making Chelsea into a vampire, but it's not that simple. You're a vampire, and you're not a bit like her. I should have seen the way she was. I feel like a fool." He frowned. "I guess everybody shows you their best side when they want you to like them. That's part of it, right? Heck, I do it myself."

"Also, Chelsea has great legs," said Rina.

James laughed. "Right. Chelsea is the vampire with the greatest legs," he teased.

"I've seen all the boys looking at them," said Rina.

"Great legs are good," said James, his eyes softening as he looked at her, "but being a nice person is even better."

"You think?"

"Believe me, I'm sure of it."

Chelsea had never thought she would be glad to get back to school, but after all the tests at the psychologist's office, school was a relief. She had even insisted to her parents that she had to come back for afternoon classes. It was funny how easily she had slipped into the routine. That morning when she had stepped out of her car and put her foot on

the pavement of the school parking lot, she had
felt like ordinary seventeen-year-old Chelsea
Hammond, a girl whose birthstone was an ame-
thyst and whose legs were her best feature. It didn't
seem to matter that she was a vampire who could
turn herself into odd shapes and cast hypnotic eyes
on victims to rob them of their will to resist. Now
that she was back at school, none of that seemed to
count. The most important thing suddenly was that
James had humiliated her in the eyes of her classmates. He had dumped her in front of a bunch of
weird kids whom she didn't even know. It drove
Chelsea crazy to think people like that were feeling
sorry for her. "I'm going to make him pay for what
he's done to me," she muttered.

In class, Chelsea's teachers made a big fuss, but
they kept looking at her in a kind of worried way.
She supposed they were afraid she was going to go
loony during class. When she got back to school
after lunch and went to English, her teacher, Mrs.
Wize, said she was glad that Chelsea was back safe
and sound, but she tottered on her high heels and
nearly stumbled backing away. Maybe, thought
Chelsea with some amusement, she thought amnesia was catching.

"You'd better take a seat," Mrs. Wize said ner-
vously. "You need to save your strength."

Chelsea grinned at her and sat down. She had
never paid much attention to the teacher before,
having better things to do with her time, but today
she found herself looking at her closely, noticing

how scrawny and little she was, with overpermed hair and a skinny neck. She was both round-shouldered and hollow chested. It was truly hard to believe that the woman had eight pints of warm blood in her.

Chelsea found herself checking out the classroom, looking for someone more nourishing. Molly grinned at her briefly, then returned to what she had been doing, writing Nathan Panovitch's name in a border around her English notebook. Molly's writing was round and full of curlicues, so the border gave the effect of a fine filigree done in ballpoint ink.

Chelsea stared at her friend, remembering that Molly always combed her hair in the rest room after English. Nathan Panovitch was in their algebra class, and the last thing Molly wanted was to have her hair looking stringy when she was trying to impress Nathan.

Laura leaned forward and whispered in Chelsea's ear. "Is it true you've got amnesia?"

Chelsea nodded. "The doctor said my memory might come back at any time—or never."

"Weird," said Laura respectfully.

"Class!" Mrs. Wize tapped on her desk with her pencil. "I know we all want to welcome Chelsea back."

The class burst out in applause. "Way to go, Chelsea!" someone yelled.

"But we've got a lot of ground to cover before the test on Friday, so let's get to work." Mrs. Wize frowned. "Now, if you will please turn to page one-oh-five of your book."

It was hard for Chelsea to keep her mind on the life of Nathaniel Hawthorne. Who cared? When Mrs. Wize started talking about *The Scarlet Letter*, all Chelsea could think about was blood. Scarlet blood.

When class was over, Chelsea stood up, smiling vaguely. Molly caught her eye and came over.

"Is it driving you crazy, everybody fussing over you?" asked Molly. "I guess they say the same things over and over again. 'Glad to have you back'—that kind of thing. It must get pretty old."

"It's okay," said Chelsea. "People are being awfully nice." *Except for James*, she reminded herself. *He's being mean.*

The two girls walked together down the hall toward the rest room. When they got there, Chelsea followed Molly inside. Water was dripping steadily into the sink, and rusty mineral stains streaked the porcelain. The two windows overhead were frosted and had crisscrossed safety wire embedded in the glass. No one could see them from outside, Chelsea realized, but she still had to worry about someone coming in. Suddenly she spotted a wedge of wood in the corner, what the janitors used to prop the door open when the place was being cleaned. Surreptitiously, she slid it with her foot so that its narrow point was forced under the door. Now it would wedge the door shut.

Molly parted her curly carroty hair, and strands

fell into her face. She blew them out of her eyes. "I hear you and James are having some problems," she said.

"We broke up." Chelsea clenched her fists. "But I'm going to get him back. You watch."

"I didn't like to mention it before—" Molly glanced at her "—but I think he got kind of tight with that new girl while you were away."

"Rina. I hate her," Chelsea said in a low voice. Her fangs stirred, and she found herself staring fixedly at Molly's throat. "Hold still, Molly!" she cried abruptly.

Molly froze, suddenly frightened. "What? Is there a bug on me?"

"Yes, right here." Chelsea lifted Molly's long hair with one hand, then bent her head and bit deeply into the soft flesh of her neck. In the mirror she saw Molly's eyes widen suddenly and her mouth fall open in shock. She would remember nothing later, Chelsea thought with satisfaction. Chelsea was able to support the entire weight of Molly's body when her knees buckled, and she lowered her gently to the tile floor. Kneeling beside her, her teeth buried in the soft flesh, Chelsea gulped down the blood, almost dizzy with pleasure.

She heard voices outside. The door strained on its hinges. "Hey, the door's stuck," somebody yelled.

"Give it another push," said a deep voice.

Chelsea snatched a paper towel from the dispenser and blotted telltale blood drops off Molly's neck. Molly lay peacefully on the tile floor, her knees bent, her mouth open. Only two small puncture marks at the base of the throat showed that a vampire had attacked her. Already a yellow bruise had formed around the marks. Glancing anxiously over her shoulder at the bulging door, Chelsea buttoned the top button of Molly's shirt to hide the marks.

"Help!" she called. "Molly's fainted."

She snatched the wooden wedge from under the door. The door flew open suddenly, and Laura and another girl lurched in off balance. Seeing Molly lying on the floor, Laura screamed.

A crowd began gathering at the door. "It's Molly!" someone yelled. "What happened? What's wrong with her?"

"She was combing her hair," said Chelsea, "and all of a sudden she passed out."

"No!" Laura cried. She was on her knees at Molly's side. "Get an ambulance, somebody!" she screamed.

Chelsea felt a flutter of fear. Had she gone too far? Was Molly dead? "I feel kind of faint, too," she said suddenly. "Maybe I'd better go sit down."

"Jeez, yes." Tom darted in, grabbed Chelsea's shoulders, and pulled her out into the hall. He looked shaken. "You've already been through enough with that amnesia and everything. Go sit down somewhere."

"Maybe it's a gas leak," someone suggested. "Carbon monoxide can take out a whole building.

All of a sudden people start dropping like flies."

Chelsea pressed through the crowd outside the door. She noticed faces around her turning green. The suggestion that the school might be filling with poison gas was spreading panic. She smiled. They would really be green, she thought, if they realized a vampire walked among them.

She went to algebra class and slid into her desk. The blackboard was covered with algebra problems. Ugh. She hated algebra.

"Are you okay, Chelsea?" Nathan Panovitch inquired anxiously. "I hear you had amnesia."

"I'm fine. It's just that I'm kind of shaken up. Molly just passed out in the girls' room."

"You're kidding me!" Nathan blanched. "Is she epileptic or something?"

Chelsea shook her head.

"On one of those crash diets, then?" he suggested. He sat down at his desk. His mouth was working anxiously. Chelsea had not noticed before that he was growing a patchy mustache. He must have started it while she was away. He gulped. "I hope it's not anything catching."

"Actually, I'm wondering if it isn't something viral," Chelsea said, glancing at him slyly.

Nathan had a wild mop of curly black hair that sat atop the shaven sides of his head. He was carelessly dressed in a baggy purple shirt and wrinkled khaki pants. Chelsea would never in a million years have figured him for a hypochondriac.

She went on, "I'm sort of wondering if it could

be mono." Seeing his alarm, her sense of mischief prompted her to add, "Or maybe one of those mysterious hantaviruses that wipe you out like that." She snapped her fingers.

Nathan gulped again. "Did you touch her?"

An ambulance siren sounded in the distance.

"Well, sure," said Chelsea. "I tried to help."

Nathan scooted his desk away from Chelsea's. "Jeez, you can't be too careful," he breathed.

Molly had at last made an indelible impression on Nathan, thought Chelsea, amused. But it wasn't quite the impression she had had in mind.

Chelsea kept an eye out for James after class, but she didn't happen to run into him in the hall. Maybe he was deliberately avoiding her. She was a little disappointed because she had been looking forward to snubbing him.

She heard later that a bunch of kids had upset stomachs after Molly was found and that all were taken to the hospital for observation. The wing was closed off to check for a gas leak. Nobody seemed to think Molly was dead, and Chelsea told herself that modern medicine was wonderful. Once they pumped Molly full of plasma she'd be as good as new. Why worry? A vampire had to eat.

When Chelsea got home from school, she found a note pinned to the fridge with magnets.

Chelsea—
    Daddy and I have gone to talk to Dr.
Morgan about your test results. A choco-

late decadence cake is on the breakfront in the living room. Help yourself, but do not leave the house. I know you don't want Daddy and me to worry, and if you go out gallivanting, we're going to be worried sick. I'm sure we can trust you about this, sweetpea. Will call if we have to be late.

Much love,
Mamma.

Chelsea sighed. Her parents were driving her crazy watching her every minute and never wanting her to go out. Already she was regretting coming home. Her favorite foods got pushed at her morning, noon, and night and she had to force them down because her parents sat staring anxiously at her the whole time. After stuffing herself with so much junk, she felt vaguely ill. She really wasn't sure how much longer she could stand living at home.

She had been telling herself she only wanted to get revenge on James, but now that she was plopped down on the bed in her room—where she allowed herself to face her most secret thoughts—she realized she actually missed him. An empty place seemed to echo inside her at the thought of him. Without James and his easygoing good humor, the world seemed a less friendly place. She loved the low sound of his voice and his long dark lashes—particularly when he was looking down at his sketchbook, and they lay like shadows against his cheeks. She even found herself missing his quiet stubbornness.

If only she could turn him into a vampire, Chelsea was sure things would be the same between them as they used to be. She tightened her lips. Things *would* be that way again, she promised herself.

She peeled off the tights she had chosen to hide her pale legs. Quickly she wiggled out of her sweater and let her short kilt fall to the floor. From the closet she took her favorite red-satin slip dress with the droopy off-the-shoulder sleeves. Slipping it over her head, she surveyed herself with satisfaction in the full-length mirror. Nice. She took Rina's bracelet out of her drawer and slipped it on her wrist. Even better. The rubies' fire leaped and danced against her pale skin. She shimmied a little in front of the mirror. If only James could see her in this, she knew he couldn't resist her. The problem was James hated school dances, so there wasn't much chance he would show up at the Autumn Fling on Saturday. But if he did come, if Rina persuaded him to, Chelsea was sure she could lure him outside alone and make him into a vampire. The red dress was a killer! She grinned.

The doorbell rang, and Chelsea caught her breath in surprise. Who could it be? Her friends always came in the back way. It must be somebody selling something. "Coming!" she screeched. Barefoot, she hurried to the front door, her long blond hair streaming loose. She threw the door open and stared, dumbfounded to see Vlad standing on the doorstep. His clothes and hair looked vaguely dusty, as if he had walked the entire distance from the airport. A slender suitcase sat beside him on the steps. "Vlad!" she exclaimed. "What a nice surprise!"

"You drove away without me, Chelsea," he said evenly. "How do you think I felt standing there on the curb with two suitcases? I felt like an idiot."

"I didn't mean to hurt your feelings—" she began.

"You didn't hurt my feelings," Vlad interrupted her. He glanced around the room. "Don't worry about that."

"I was hoping to meet up with you again." Chelsea forced a smile. "We made a great team, didn't we? But there were some things I needed to take care of right away at home, and I was afraid you wouldn't understand."

Vlad folded his arms across his chest and looked at her with amusement. "You wanted to meet up with me again, huh? So, exactly how were you going to do that?"

"Well, I know where you live," said Chelsea, improvising. She didn't truly think Vlad planned to go on living in the tumbledown shack in the woods where he had taken her to teach her vampire tricks. But it was the best line she could think of on the spur of the moment.

Vlad laughed. "You are hilarious, Chelsea."

"You think so?" She blinked. She hated his superior laugh. She had suspected for some time that Vlad thought she was stupid just because she didn't read books the way he did.

He sat down on the couch. "I taught you every vampire trick you know," he pointed out. "Didn't I?"

"Yes, and I'm really grateful," said Chelsea.

"You wouldn't know how to do a thing if it weren't for me. You were helpless when I first met you. Remember how you were talking about finding a dentist to file down your fangs?"

"You're mad at me," Chelsea said accusingly.

"Nah!"

"Yes, you are. I can tell by your tone of voice."

"Okay, I'm a little bit ticked about the way you drove off and left me," he admitted.

"So why did you come looking for me if you're mad at me?"

"Actually, since you ask, I'm kind of short of cash." He extended his hand.

Chelsea groped for her purse on the couch and held out some bills.

He counted them. "Is that the best you can do? You were winning big in Vegas."

"Most of it's in the bank," she lied. Rolls of money were hidden in her underwear drawer, but she had no intention of sharing them with Vlad.

"What's that?" he snapped. Suddenly he grabbed her wrist.

She blinked at him in bewilderment. "What?"

"What's this on your wrist?"

Chelsea glanced at her hand. "A bracelet. That's all. I stole it."

"From whom?" he hissed.

"From Rina. She's the one who made me into a vampire."

"Rina's here?" Vlad's eyes looked strangely blank for an instant.

"You know her?"

"Know her!" He smiled. "You might say we go way back. I'm the one who made *her* into a vampire!"

"Maybe you'd like to kill her," suggested Chelsea hopefully. "It might be a special treat for you—if you like killing vampires, I mean."

Vlad smiled. "Maybe. You're a sweet little thing, aren't you?"

She smiled. "Actually, I guess we're kind of alike."

"We both like to have a good time." He showed a flash of white teeth. "Vegas?"

"It was fun," agreed Chelsea.

"We both like to have our own way, too, huh?" Vlad smiled. "I suppose you can't wait to tell me where Rina lives."

"She lives on Oak Street," Chelsea said promptly. "You'll recognize her house right away. It's big and old-fashioned like a haunted mansion. You know, the kind you see a lot of at Halloween? Well, maybe you don't know about Halloween, coming from another country and everything. I'm not sure they have it in Transylvania or wherever it is you're from. Let me write down directions to her house." She reached for a pen. "I'm really glad we found each other again, Vlad. Let's make a date. You can pick me up at eight. We'll have supper and a good talk afterward."

"Ye-es," he said, smiling. "Perhaps we could share someone." He lifted her hand and pressed his lips to her flesh. "Pigeon-blood rubies," he whispered. "My favorite." He brushed her skin with his lips and then stood up. "Until tonight, my little cabbage leaf."

As soon as he left, Chelsea leaped to her feet. "Really!" she breathed. "He is completely over the top. I *hate* that accent. And the laugh! Yuck. It's time for me to get out of here." She was sick of living at home anyway, she reminded herself. What was she waiting for? Rina might be able to protect James by sticking to his side every minute at school, but she wasn't staying in his bedroom with him. It would be dark soon. Chelsea realized that the thing for her to do was go over to the Ryders' house right now and make James into a vampire at once. Then, while he was still weak and confused, she could bundle him into her car and drive away.

The phone rang, and Chelsea pounced on it. "Hello?"

It was Trip's mother, and she sounded frantic.

"No, Mrs. Davis, I haven't seen him since last night." Chelsea listened in silence as Trip's mother recounted how she had called the hospitals and the highway patrol and had turned Trip's name in to the police as a missing person. "That's awful!"

cried Chelsea. "I hope nothing bad has happened to him."

Mrs. Davis rambled on for several minutes before Chelsea managed to cut her off. "I'm sorry," she insisted. "I just don't have a clue where he could be. I wish I could help." She hung up and glanced out the dining room window. Trip's car was parked in her back driveway, and the keys must have vaporized with Trip when he burned, so there was no way she could move it. The sooner she got out of town the better.

6

At Rina's house, a man in overalls and a windbreaker stood on a tall ladder, affixing a large, rigid awning. Vlad noticed they were the sort of awnings that could be lowered and fastened over windows to protect the glass during storms—he had seen them on the Riviera. Somehow he doubted that storm protection was what Rina had in mind. It looked to him as if she was making her house tight against vampires. The men must have been working for some time, because awnings were already fixed to all the other windows.

"Is that the last one?" a man on the ground called.

"I think so. Check the truck."

A man with a ruler stuck in his belt hopped up in the truck, which was marked MILTON'S SHUTTER AND AWNING. "That's it," he called. "Let's pack it up."

When the workmen had driven away, Vlad

stepped out of his hiding place in the woods and deliberately paced the perimeter of the house. If he could slip in the house unseen, he could surprise Rina. His sharp eyes noticed that a stout new door looked as if it had been installed recently. A dusting of sawdust showed on its sill. Rina was behaving as if she were afraid of someone. Chelsea, perhaps? After all, she couldn't possibly know yet that he was in town. Vlad smiled. When all was said and done, it was probably easier to knock at her door than to try to break in. Before she had even recovered from the surprise of seeing him, he could lay his hands on either side of her neck, stun her with his gaze, and bring her under his power again. Why not?

Purple shadows were lengthening on Rina's well-kept lawn, and the sky had turned the deep lavender of dusk. Vlad felt the money Chelsea had given him wadded up in his pocket. What he needed, he decided, were new clothes. He didn't want to show up at Rina's place in travel-worn jeans. It hit him suddenly that he ought to get Chelsea to teach him how to drive. Then maybe he would buy a car. All the American teenagers he saw had them, and he was sick of hitchhiking. He wanted his own wheels.

As he walked, shadows deepened and the streetlights came on. At last he saw the moon rise in a dark sky. He stepped off the sidewalk into the shadow of a tree, clenched his hands tightly, took a deep breath, and focused his mind until his eyes felt warm and full. He felt them bulge until he could see in all directions at once. His arms and hands grew glossy and green. Then he rubbed his hands together, watching them become thin and black with sparse, ragged black hairs. He knew he must be bald and he rubbed his stick hands self-consciously against his bare green skull. It was an awkward stage of the metamorphosis, but soon he would be done. He could feel his mouth pursing as his body contracted. The air around him gave a sucking sound as he shrank. He saw that he was now dwarfed by the ragweed along the sidewalk. The tree's branches seemed as far away as the stars. He crouched in a ragweed jungle, and its rank smell made him feel punchy. His body vibrated with a strange and directionless buzzing, and he realized his wings were singing. He rose in the air, a glossy-green blowfly. Buzzing loudly, he flew in an erratic path toward Golden Leaf Mall.

"Do you want to put them on here?" asked the clerk. She was a plump and enthusiastic young woman with short blond hair. Over her jeans she wore a voluminous pink coverall with the name of the shop embroidered in script on the pocket. "You can use that counter over there, if you like," she added.

"Thank you," said Rina. She sat down at the Formica counter next to a sink and carefully inserted the contact lenses. She was relieved that the brown lenses did not make everything in the shop look odd. But it wouldn't have mattered if they had. Rina would have stared at a brown world forever for James's sake. She was determined to do all she possibly could to make herself look more human so that he would love her.

Rina reached into the shopping bag at her feet and fingered the bunches of bright ribbons hidden there. The feel of the satin comforted her as much as if they had been magic talismans. When she was alive, she had braided bright ribbons into her hair on market days, when she had walked to the village to see her friends. Strange to think how long it had been since she had thought of those friends. But since she had met James, she realized, her sweet memories of that former life had grown steadily stronger. Now she thought often of her father's inn and the good smell of her mother's bread. She had loved sunshine when it sparkled in the morning dew and made her hair and her ribbons glow with color. The memory of those days was strong, and their happiness seemed close to her. It was almost as if she could reach for it with both hands and hold it.

But the feeling was an illusion. She was a vampire. Now on sunlit days, she was better off at places like this mall, where the sun's rays never penetrated.

"So, how are those lenses working for you?" asked the clerk.

"Perfect," gulped Rina. "I love them." She stumbled to her feet, grabbed her purse, and clutched her shopping bag in the other hand. "Thank you very much," she added. The shop walls were mirrored and her image was reflected back at her tenfold. She looked small and pale next to the pink-cheeked clerk, but Rina was relieved that she showed up at all in the mirror. Vlad had once boasted that his grandfather's heart had grown so cold that his image had disappeared from mirrors. Rina had found the story terrifying. She didn't want her vampire nature to overcome her and devour her heart.

Rina hesitated at the door to the shop, wondering which way to turn. She wanted to avoid going by the fountain at the heart of the mall. Even looking at the fast-rushing water made her feel she was losing her strength. She was wondering whether she should go toward the display of earrings or in the direction of the cookie shop, when suddenly an eerily familiar figure walked past. She gasped and recoiled.

"Are you all right?" asked the clerk, hurrying toward her.

Rina clutched her hand to her pounding heart. "N-no. I mean, yes. I'm fine, really."

"Are you sure? We had a lady pass out here last week, and I sure don't want that happening again."

Rina licked her lips. Her gaze was still fastened on Vlad as he walked away. He carried his head high and had a way of moving that was both proud and graceful, like a dancer. But how could he be here in North Carolina? She hadn't seen him since the stormy night many years ago when she had left him tossing green-faced on his cot in his stateroom. She had gone out on deck and dived overboard into the black sea. With her leather bag strapped to her waist she had swum desperately to the nearby shore. She was a strong swimmer, even without her vampire powers. But remembering it now, she felt almost ill with fear. Swimming in a stormy sea at night, she had been taking a big risk. Yet somehow she had survived—and the risk had been worth it to be free of Vlad. She blinked rapidly, forcing her thoughts back to the present.

The clerk was gazing at her with concern. "Are you *sure* you're all right?" she asked.

"Oh, yes, I'm fine, thank you," murmured Rina. She smiled at the kind clerk and darted out of the store.

Moving on silent feet, she glided to a nearby ficus tree. She put her shopping bag down on the tile floor and peered out from behind the ficus leaves. The dark boy had stopped at the earring display that stood about twenty feet away. He was checking out the racks of pierced earrings, twirling the carousel with one hand. Doubt grew in Rina's heart. Her memories of her past life had been so strong lately that she wondered if they had colored her perceptions. How could this boy possibly be Vlad? Yet it looked like him, with the same olive complexion and dark hair.

Rina was tempted to change form to get closer. She glanced around. Nearby a couple of elderly women were coming out of a shoe store. Some kids in leather jackets were standing in a tight circle, talking. A toddler chased a red balloon past her. Someone would notice if she changed form here in the middle of the mall. Besides, she was so rattled, she wasn't even certain she could summon the concentration she would need to do it. Instead she pricked her ears and strained to hear what the dark boy said.

"Do you have anything with a ruby stone?" The boy's teeth gleamed in a smile. To Rina's relief he didn't glance in her direction. "A bloodred color is what I'd prefer," he added.

The girl at the counter had masses of curly blond hair. Rina saw her tousled head dip below the counter and then rise again. Evidently she was getting something out of the glass case where the more expensive earrings were kept.

Rina stared. The boy's voice had been unmistakably like Vlad's, a kind of honeyed rasp. Besides, he seemed to have a slight accent, as if English were not his native tongue. She might be wrong, of course. She hadn't heard Vlad speak in many years, she reminded herself.

"Ah," said the boy, lifting a pair of glittering red earrings. "These are nice. How much?"

The girl mumbled something Rina couldn't make out.

Suddenly the boy put down the earrings and laid his hands on either side of the girl's throat. Then Rina heard her say in a clear, loud monotone, "I can offer you a very special deal. Only five dollars. That's a ninety percent discount."

It was Vlad all right. He had bewitched the clerk to get a better price on the earrings. That was just like him. He laid spells casually here and there in a lighthearted, mischievous manner.

A chill froze Rina's heart. If Vlad found her, she was sure he would try to put a spell on her, too. He might even succeed. And what if he discovered he had a rival in James? He would kill James without a thought.

Rina had seen all she needed to. Her heart pounding with fear, she slipped out of the mall.

In moments, her car was speeding through the dark streets to her house. Every instinct in her shrieked *Run!*

She ran upstairs to her room. The smell of ashes hung in the room, and she shuddered when she saw the scorched rug where Trip had burned. She hastily rolled the rug up and slid it against the wall. Poor Trip! He had never had a chance against a vampire as ruthless as Chelsea.

Rina began tossing clothes into a suitcase. Only two dim thoughts were in her head: She had to get away from Vlad. And before she left, she must say good-bye to James.

James stood at the door of his sister's vacant room, taking in the familiar clutter. Tennis rackets, pennants, and bright posters hung on the walls. A plush purple hippopotamus and a white unicorn stood next to the CD player, and beside the bed was something James hadn't noticed in a long time: a crude wooden frame, laced with a web of delicate strings, some with beads and feathers strung on them. A dream catcher. Native Americans made them to catch good dreams. James hoped that wherever Susan's spirit was, she had caught up with her dreams. He touched a feather gently and wondered what Susan would think of Rina. Somehow he thought they would have liked each other.

He closed the door quietly behind him. As he stepped into the hall, he froze. Chelsea's voice came floating up the stairs.

"I won't stay long," she said. "I just want to give James his CD back."

The cheerful lilt to her tone chilled his blood. He had thought of everything. The windows were closed tight. The space around the pipes was sealed. He had even checked to make sure the fireplace flue was closed. Why hadn't it occurred to him that Chelsea would come to the front door of the house and ask to come in? It would never occur to his family to bar Chelsea's way. He had been so stupid not to warn them!

James ran into his bedroom and locked the door, but he knew the door would not hold Chelsea long if she was determined to get in. The lock was only a flimsy push-button device. Night had fallen, and she would have her full vampire strength. He had not forgotten how easily Rina had picked him up and got him to a place of safety the night Chelsea showed up unexpectedly at Molly's séance.

He heard a banging on the door. "James? Open up! I'm not mad at you anymore. I just want to give you back your CD. No hard feelings." The doorknob rattled impatiently.

Right, thought James. *No hard feelings. All I want to do is make you into a vampire.*

He slid the window open silently and threw a leg over the sill. Breathing hard, he squeezed out the window and slipped onto the roof. He had climbed out on the roof once when he was ten and had gotten grounded for three weeks for the escapade. Somehow when he was ten it had seemed like fun, but tonight his breath was coming in fast gulps.

The moon shone on the shingles, making them look treacherously smooth. He felt sheer terror when his foot slipped a little. Luckily he was wearing sneakers or he would have slid right down. He swallowed hard as he carefully shifted his position to get a grip on the dormer window's roof. When he had a firm hold, he carefully edged around the side of the dormer. Clinging to it, he crouched beside it, waiting.

He heard a sharp bang. His bedroom door had been flung rudely open.

"James!" Chelsea's voice floated thinly out the window. James started when movement caught his eye, but it was only the white curtain billowing out the open window. Immediately after, though, a blond head poked out the window. James's foot slipped a little, and for a heart-stopping moment, he froze. Not far away from him, Chelsea's long hair blew in the breeze. It whipped around her head, so he could not see her face. She seemed to be wearing a dark-red sweater, and she was so uncharacteristically silent, James was certain she was listening for sounds of movement. To his own ears his breath seemed to whistle as loudly as a typhoon, but mercifully the wind drowned him out. Leaves rattled noisily down the shingles, and the branches of the oak tree creaked. James clung desperately to his perch, and finally Chelsea withdrew. He heard the door to his bedroom slam shut, but he was afraid to creep back into his room. The slamming of the door could be a trick.

Squinting against the wind, he peered into the chill darkness, wondering what to do next. Chelsea's Mazda was parked in the driveway behind his car. He could not imagine what she must be saying to his mother.

As James peered into the darkness, he saw headlights move down the dark street, flickering as they passed along the avenue of trees. Rina's gray Lincoln glided up under the streetlight, and for a moment he thought she would to pull into his driveway. But though the car hesitated near the curb, it didn't turn in. He realized that Rina must have spotted Chelsea's Mazda and had second thoughts about coming up the driveway.

This was the time to make a break for it. He

ran down the sloping roof, his feet slipping frighteningly. He knew he must be making an incredible racket that anyone would hear if they were in the rooms just under him. He slowed short of the edge of the roof, afraid momentum would carry him over, and froze for a moment, listening to his heart beating. A distant train whistle sounded in the night. He thought he could hear the low murmur of rain. Slowly, he inched up to the edge. Getting a firm grip with his soles, he pushed off and leaped for the oak. Branches hit him in the face and scratched his hands and arms. He struggled to catch hold of something—anything. At last, he got a slippery grasp on bark and managed to brace his foot against solid wood. He peered down. The ground seemed far away. Carefully, he inched his way lower on the limbs. He could see Rina's headlights flickering through the thick branches. Her car was now moving, and he was afraid she would drive away without seeing him. Suddenly he let loose and slipped to the ground, landing with a thud that rattled his teeth.

As if it were a mirage, the gray Lincoln glided up to the curb near him. James lunged for it and jerked the door open. "Chelsea is inside!" he gasped. "She's after me!" His palms were scraped and burning as he slid in the car and slammed the door shut.

"Oh, James!" Rina sobbed. "I was so worried. I saw her car and didn't know what you would want me to do."

"It's okay, Rina. You did fine. Just drive."
James could feel tension in every muscle as he
cast a glance over his shoulder. Through the trees
he could make out a white metallic glimmer in
the driveway. Chelsea's car was parked there, but
that meant nothing since he had to assume
Chelsea could turn into a bat as easily as Rina
could. She could be flying after them right now
on silent wings. He was glad Rina had all her car
windows shut.

A sudden thought froze his blood. "Jeez, Rina,
you don't think she'll go after my mother or Danny
do you? Maybe we ought to go back."

Rina shook her head. "I don't think Chelsea's
hungry," she said. "Actually, I have an idea she fed
this afternoon at school. She wants *you*, James."

"Great!" he said bitterly. "So what am I going to
do? She just came in the house and marched right
up to my room. I wish I'd warned my mother.
Maybe I couldn't tell her Chelsea is a vampire, but
I could have told her *something*. I guess Chelsea's
in the house right now, telling lies. . . ." He glanced
at Rina. "What do you mean, she fed this afternoon? What happened?"

"Didn't you hear that Molly passed out in the
rest room? Somebody told me that Chelsea was
with her."

James groaned. "Molly! Jeez, Rina, they were
friends." He stared at her, his face suddenly rigid.
"She didn't *do* anything to Molly, did she?"

Rina shook her head. "Oh, I don't think so. I

heard the rescue squad came for Molly, and they rushed her to the hospital. If Chelsea had turned her into a vampire, I don't think she would have let the medics take her to the hospital." Rina avoided his eyes. "They might find out strange things when they did tests, you see. Vampires don't have human blood."

James buried his face in his hands. "This is unbelievable. It's just unreal, that's all. What am I supposed to do?"

"Well, you can wait until Chelsea's left your house," Rina suggested, "and then you can go home and tell your family not to let Chelsea in the house anymore."

"Why won't she leave me alone?" asked James bitterly. "Why doesn't she get out of town? All I used to hear about was how she couldn't wait to get away from Tyler Falls. What's stopping her?"

"You, probably."

"Great!"

"I guess she's mad at you and wants to kill you. Or maybe she wants to make you into a vampire because she thinks that's the way to make sure you two will be close again."

"You'd think it'd cross her mind," he said, "that if she makes me into a vampire, I might just get closer to you instead of to her."

Rina smiled at him timorously. "I guess when people are in love, they can fool themselves."

"Chelsea's not in love with me," said James. "She just wants to have some kind of power over me." He shivered as he gazed out the window. They were out of the neighborhood now and on the highway that formed the main east–west corridor of the town.

A fine mist had fogged the windshield. Rina switched on the wipers. Water hissed under the car's wheels. "James, I've got to leave town," she said suddenly. She shot him a frightened look. "That's why I came over. So I could say good-bye. I'm already packed. My stuff is in the trunk."

James was suddenly terrified of losing her. He glanced at her. "What's going on, Rina?"

"Vlad is in town. You remember Vlad?"

James winced. He remembered Vlad perfectly. The creep that had made Rina into a vampire and had given her the ruby bracelet. The guy she used to *love*.

"Yeah," he said shortly. "I remember him. I thought you two hadn't been in touch. How did he find out where you were living?"

"I don't know!" Rina wailed. "But I've got to get away."

"Why?" asked James. Now that his fears had been stirred, anything seemed possible. He looked at Rina. "If you don't care about the guy anymore, Rina, what's it to you what he does?"

"I *don't* care about him!" Rina cried. "But he's possessive. If he finds out how I feel about you, he might kill you. And if I don't go away with him, he might kill me, too. He's selfish!"

"Jeez, he should hook up with Chelsea," said

James. "They'd make a great pair. What a bunch of sweethearts."

"I'm afraid of him," said Rina in a small voice.

James slid down in the seat. "I think you and me had better go visit Gram."

"Okay," said Rina. She glanced at him. "But who is Gram?"

"My mother's mother, Nancy Fenner—a very nice lady who runs a horseback riding stable in the mountains." If he and Rina could stay out of town long enough, James thought, somehow the situation might improve. It sure couldn't get much worse.

James was surprised to find his spirits lifting a little. He dimly realized that at the root of his optimism was the cheerful conviction that Rina really didn't care about Vlad, but he was not prone to examine his thoughts too carefully. Getting out of town was the main thing.

"Has it occurred to you," James darted a glance at Rina, "that Vlad and Chelsea may have already taken up with each other? Didn't you say that somebody must have been teaching Chelsea vampire tricks? After all, she was missing from town for ten days."

Rina's eyes widened.

"It's just an idea," said James.

"We have to escape!" cried Rina. "Oh, James, it's so much nicer with you going along with me. I thought I was going to have to go off by myself and be lonely forever." She choked on a sob.

James slid his arm around her shoulders. "Hey, no! Calm down, Rina!" He hated to imagine what his grandmother was going to think about Rina, but he pushed that uncomfortable thought from his mind. "I'll just call my mom from somewhere along the road and let her know I'm all right."

"James?" Rina darted a shy smile his way. "This makes me so happy. With you along, it won't seem like running away at all."

James wanted to see her happy, but a small pessimistic voice in his mind could not be stilled: *Yeah, it's great. Except for the slight problem about what to tell my grandmother about me showing up with a strange girl—and the very big problem that the girl happens to be a vampire.*

7

Chelsea could have wept with frustration. She checked James's room carefully, even the closet and under the bed. While she was at it, she looked around upstairs, checking the other bedrooms and the bathroom. Then she tripped lightly down the stairs. "He's not there," she reported.

Mrs. Ryder frowned. "Are you sure?"

"I looked around upstairs," said Chelsea. "No sign of him." She smiled tightly. "I guess he didn't believe me when I said no hard feelings. He must have sneaked out the window and jumped off the roof to get away from me."

"Oh, Chelsea, don't be ridiculous. He must have gone out before you got here, and I just didn't hear him leave." Mrs. Ryder opened the front door and glanced outside. "That's odd. His car is still in the driveway. In fact, your car has blocked his in." She opened the door wider, and her expression became guarded. "Oh, well, just give the CD to me, dear, and I'll see that James gets it. It was nice of you to come by."

Chelsea could see the idea almost visibly dawning in Mrs. Ryder's mind that James had wanted to get away from his ex-girlfriend desperately enough to slip out the upstairs window. Now Mrs. Ryder was obviously eager to get rid of Chelsea so that she could go check and see if James had fallen and broken his neck in his eagerness to escape.

"Yeah." Chelsea laid the CD down on the piano. "Well, do tell him I came by, okay?" She slipped outside. Her vampire strength was like a coiled spring pressing against her chest, and she could feel her fangs stirring. How she longed to bury her teeth in James's soft flesh! She found herself thinking bitterly that this was just like him. Even when they were going together, it had seemed he was always refusing to do what she wanted.

A fine rain had begun to fall, and she stood silently by her car, letting the mist bead in her hair. She would have to move her car, of course. Mrs. Ryder was standing at the door, watching her. Chelsea knew she had to make a show of backing out of the driveway, but she didn't have to go far. James must be around in the yard or the neighborhood somewhere. He couldn't have gotten far without a car.

Chelsea backed out and let her car glide up the street until she was out of sight of the house. Then she got out and let her essence unwind in the gusty wetness of the night as she returned to the house.

By the time she got there, she was no more than a shifting pattern of light and shadow and was almost invisible. Her steps were so weightless that they did not rustle the damp leaves. She stood unseen as Mrs. Ryder walked past her wearing a hooded windbreaker. "James?" Mrs. Ryder's voice floated on the breeze, and the older woman's steps sounded on the fallen leaves. Chelsea stood silently in a puddle on the bare ground under the big oak, watching as Mrs. Ryder's hood fell off when she lifted her face to scan the roof for her missing son. "James?" she called. The beam of a flashlight played among the shrubs near the house.

Chelsea caught a whiff of James's scent clinging to the oak, but the night was so windy and wet that she soon lost it. She could have wept with annoyance. Where could he be hiding? Mrs. Ryder seemed to be going around to the other side of the house. Chelsea could still hear her, but her voice was fainter.

A few minutes later a small bat flew around the house. The bat looped and dipped near the streetlight as if to catch the insects drawn by its glow. Its tiny eyes glowed with a strange intelligence in the snub-nosed furry face, and when it opened its mouth, it showed a flash of white fangs. "Chelsea," it hissed softly so as not to forget her name. It perched in the oak, hanging from its hooklike claws, and turned its head curiously. Its ears were tuned to hear the faintest rustle, but all it heard was rain and blowing leaves. James's scent clung to the bark, but it seemed clear now that his trail disappeared at the foot of the tree. The bat released its grip on the tree branch and flapped its wings tirelessly as it circled the house, checking for any signs of movement. She heard the door close as James's mother went back inside the house, and she swooped under the oak, settling awkwardly on the wet ground. The old oak shuddered as if it had been struck, and in a moment a dark and formless shadow slipped from under its canopy. The strange shadow slid along the sidewalk to Chelsea's parked car. *James must be with Rina*, she thought. *He has to be*. As the thought formed with perfect clearness in her mind, the shadow grew more solid and began unmistakably to resemble Chelsea.

Chelsea opened her car door and slid in behind the wheel, sick that she had missed her chance. She had hoped to catch James alone in his room. Had she been able to corner him there, she could have turned him into a vampire. She giggled at the thought and hastily covered her mouth with her hand. But she had missed her chance. Her face darkened in disappointment.

She knew she couldn't go home. Her parents would have already checked her room and discovered she had packed up her things. Probably they were busy freaking out at this very moment. If she went back home, they'd watch her so closely it would be like being in jail. And besides, they must be wondering why Trip's car was parked in the back driveway. Nothing but trouble was waiting for her at home. She needed to get away.

Suddenly she realized she couldn't face leaving town by herself. What had happened to her wonderful plan of turning all her friends into vampires so that they could be together? She wished she had turned Molly into a vampire while she had the chance. If only Laura hadn't been pounding on the bathroom door, she might have had time. Then she would have someone to keep her company. Why did everybody keep messing up her plans? Nothing was going right! Chelsea regretted setting Trip on fire. He would have been company, at least. Even better, he would have been a help. He could have held off Rina while she attacked James. But why did James have to like Rina in the first place?

She rested her forehead on the steering wheel. "I hate him!" she sobbed.

A few minutes later, Chelsea sat in her parked car and stared moodily out of the car's rain-streaked windows at Rina's house. The rain swept the darkness, its steady diagonal showing in the beam of her headlights.

She got out of the car and picked her way over the sodden leaves that clogged the street. Rain gurgled in the gutters. She had to know for sure if James and Rina were together. The memory of James's caresses cut her painfully now that she imagined Rina taking her place. She could picture Rina blowing in James's face and laughing, the way she herself had done. She could imagine Rina's high arched foot groping for his under a table. Perhaps at this very moment they were sitting on the couch in Rina's living room, their lips pressed together. The image of them together was so strong in Chelsea's mind that she found herself drawn almost against her will through the blowing rain. The wet grass brushed against her shoes until they were soaked, but she could not collect her wits enough to dematerialize. Instead, she clung damply to the window of the living room and peered in.

"Hello." A rasping voice spoke in her ear and Chelsea jumped.

"Vlad!" she gasped.

His curly hair was like an unruly halo in the dampness, and the light shed by the window pointed up his high cheekbones and made his eyes deep pools of darkness. He looked like an evil angel. "I thought we had a date," he said. "At eight."

She glanced at her watch. Beads of moisture had formed on the watch's crystal, and she had to squint to make out the numbers. "It's not eight yet."

"Quarter of. And it doesn't look to me as if you're in any hurry to rush home and get ready."

Vlad was wearing what looked like a brand-new suede bomber jacket. The buff-colored suede was streaked with rain. She supposed he had bought it with the money she had given him. A ruby earring winked in one earlobe. "Wait a minute!" she cried. "You're not exactly rushing over to my house to pick me up, either!"

He smiled self-consciously. "I was sort of

waiting around for Rina to show up, actually."

"Rina!" She stomped her foot in a puddle, and a shower of drops drenched her leg. "Why is everybody so crazy about Rina? What is the deal?"

Vlad shrugged. "Who can explain these things?"

"Don't give me that!" Chelsea said impatiently. "Talk sense."

"So, who else has a thing about Rina?" asked Vlad casually. "Is this boy a vampire? Perhaps I will kill him."

"No, you don't! James belongs to me."

"It sounds to me as if he belongs to Rina." Vlad laughed.

Chelsea slapped him hard.

He held a hand to his cheek and surveyed her ruefully. "Reason number one why I like Rina: She never slapped me. Not once."

"Oh, shut up," snapped Chelsea. "If you're still waiting for Rina, I guess that means they're not here. Where can they be?"

"I *was* waiting for her," Vlad amended, "but a minute ago I broke into the house, and from what I can see, it looks like she's taken off." He frowned. "I don't understand why she's in such a hurry to get out of town. And all these security precautions around the house: new door, new security awnings . . . She can't know that I've showed up. You haven't told her, have you? No, I can see you haven't." Vlad smiled. "Can it be you she's afraid of?"

"I hope so," said Chelsea. "I hope she's terrified. If they're not here, I don't know why we're standing here in the cold rain. Let's at least get in my car."

An idea was forming in her mind, and as she and Vlad slogged through the wet grass to the car, she turned it over and examined it from every angle. She didn't see any serious drawbacks.

"Vlad," she began, "I've got an idea. See what you think." She opened the car door and slid in behind the wheel. Reaching across the seat, she opened his door for him, and he got in.

Vlad made an attempt to smooth his springy hair with both hands, then he laughed and leaned back against the seat. "You want him and I want her," he said, smiling. "Let's join forces?"

"You read my mind!" she exclaimed.

"Yes," he said. "I can do that sometimes. Can't you?"

"No." Chelsea frowned. "Anyway, not yet."

Vlad smiled. "You need imagination. It helps to be able to guess how somebody else might think and feel."

"If you're so smart, tell me how you can be sure Rina's taken off," Chelsea demanded.

Vlad shook his head. "No mental telepathy needed. The bureau drawer in her room was open, and it looked like she'd been throwing clothes out of it in a big hurry. I found a box of maps in the kitchen, and the box was half empty. My guess is she's hit the highway. Maybe she doesn't plan to come back. Not anytime soon, anyway."

"But she left the lights on inside," protested Chelsea.

Vlad smiled. "No, I turned the lights on."

"How did you get in?"

"Broke a window." He shrugged. "It's simple, but it works."

"James must be with her! But I just can't see him taking off without telling his mother."

"Unless he was really scared."

"Is that some kind of slam?" asked Chelsea hotly. "Am I going to hear it again how Rina is sweet, and I'm some kind of monster?"

"Maybe the two of them aren't together," suggested Vlad. "Maybe this James is out with another girl. Or maybe he went out for a sandwich and will be back shortly."

"Oh, they're together, all right," Chelsea said bitterly. "I know it. I guess he panicked when he heard me coming in the house. I should have been sneakier. It just never occurred to me that he would dive out the window. I figured he was trapped. I did check around the house and picked up his scent on the tree outside his window, but then I lost it."

"Cars," sighed Vlad, "That's the problem with following scents these days. Even a werewolf can't track somebody who's in a car."

"But his car was still in the driveway!"

Vlad smiled. "But couldn't he be in Rina's car?"

"He must be." Chelsea spoke through clenched teeth. "I just know they're together. I can feel it in my bones. I can *see* it." Chelsea pounded her fist on the steering wheel. "Where could they have gone?"

"I was hoping you could tell me that. You know this country, Chelsea. Where would such an oddly matched couple run away to? New York, maybe? New Orleans? No one would look twice at a vampire–human match in a big, cosmopolitan city, I suppose."

"Or maybe Rina's already made him into a vampire," said Chelsea sharply.

Vlad shook his head. "I don't know James, but I know Rina. If she loves him, she would never make him into a vampire. She has a very soft heart."

"I don't know why she wouldn't do it!" snapped Chelsea. "Being a vampire is good enough for you and me. I don't have any complaints. I'm sure James would love being a vampire if he gave it a try."

Vlad smiled. "But maybe James is like Rina. Is he soft?"

"Too soft for his own good."

"People like that are made to be human," suggested Vlad. "And we are made to prey upon them." He smiled, and Chelsea could see his sharp fangs.

8

"As soon as we get to the next rest stop," said James, "I've got to call my mother. When she finds out I've gone and my car's still parked in the driveway, she's going to worry herself sick."

"Maybe she'll think you took a long walk," Rina suggested.

"Sure. I always take long walks at night in the pouring rain."

"You used to."

James was silent. He realized Rina was right. Only weeks ago, his sister's grave had drawn him like a magnet late at night and in all weather. Hadn't he met Rina there on a night like tonight? He remembered sitting by Susan's grave with Rina while the rain plastered his hair to his head and lightning bleached the landscape in short bursts. Maybe that was when his strange connection with her had been forged. From the start he had felt she could understand his unhappiness in a way that the other kids at school couldn't.

He cleared his throat uncomfortably. "I was kind of in bad shape then, I guess."

"You wanted to talk to your sister, you missed her so much."

"Yeah. It was bad."

"It's good you're forgetting how unhappy you were."

James glanced at her uneasily. "I know what *I* was doing in the cemetery, Rina. But I've never asked, what were *you* doing there?" He was sorry as soon as the words were out of his mouth. With Rina, it was better not to ask questions. If she started talking about digging up graves to get at bodies, he was afraid he would jump out of the car.

"I like the old cemetery," she said, keeping her eyes on the road ahead. He saw in the light reflected from the dashboard that tears were sparkling in her eyes.

"What's wrong?" he asked, reaching for her hand. "What's the matter?"

"You know the way the big old tree in the middle of the cemetery makes the ground heave and the gravestones buckle?" She shot him a quick glance. "It's like the tree is full of life. It seems to be trying to wake the dead."

James gazed out the rain-blurred window. "Yeah," he said. "Yeah, I see."

"Looking at that old graveyard used to make me feel as if anything were possible—as if time could go backward and the dead could awake. . . ."

"And vampires could turn into humans," James finished for her.

Rina didn't answer. She didn't have to.

James gave her knee a squeeze. He wished he could make it better for her. His heart ached with the pitiful hopelessness of it. He longed to get his hands around that creep Vlad's neck and make him suffer for what he'd done to Rina.

Rina was too thin, he thought. Not much more than bone.

But maybe it was one of those things she couldn't help because she was a vampire. He wondered uneasily if she needed blood. It even crossed his mind that he ought to offer her some of his, but he closed his eyes and forced himself to take some deep breaths. *Get a grip,* he told himself. *Some things you can't do anything about. Let go. Be reasonable. Just put one foot in front of the other, and let tomorrow take care of itself.* It was almost easier, he realized with a wry smile, when Chelsea was hot on his heels. It concentrated his attention amazingly, and he didn't have time to think about anything else.

"Pull into this rest stop," he said. "I'll drive for a while."

The car slowed, and Rina turned into the rest area. The plaza had stone benches and an elaborate planting of pansies, now dark and bedraggled with rain. Overhead, lights struggled to beam light through the drifting rain. Mist had formed a halo around them.

James groped in his pocket for change. "Sit tight," he told Rina. "I'm going to give my mother a call."

He found the pay phones under the plaza overhang, next to the bathrooms. His coins made a clunking sound as he dropped them in. He pressed the receiver to his ear. It was cold, and wet with mist. Nearby, the door to the men's bathroom was propped open, and a large pail and mop stood at its entrance. Travelers bundled up against the damp stepped around the bucket. The tile flooring under the overhang where James stood was muddy and covered with fragments of dead leaves.

"Hello?" said his mother's voice.

"Hi, Mom."

"James!" she cried. "Where are you?"

James closed his eyes and let his mother tell him about Chelsea's attempt to return his CD earlier in the evening. "What did you mean, climbing out the window like that?" she demanded. "I was afraid you'd broken your neck! Danny and I went around the entire house twice with flashlights, looking for you."

"I'm sorry. I know I should have mentioned this before," he said cautiously, "but Chelsea didn't exactly come over to return a CD. I never lent her a CD. Think about it, Mom. She listens to country-and-western. I don't. She came looking for me because, well, she wants to kill me."

A squawked *"What?"* from the receiver made him hold it away from his ear for a moment.

"I think she's gone completely around the bend," he explained patiently. Telling his mother lies was no more difficult than writing a story for English class. It was easy, once he got into the swing of it. A lot easier, in fact, than telling the plain, unvarnished truth. "Maybe she's got some kind of brain damage or something," he suggested. "Remember how she disappeared all of a sudden? Just dropped out of sight? Then she comes back claiming she's got amnesia, and the next thing I know, she's threatening to kill me. I figured it was safer for me to get out of there. I don't want to end up featured in some gruesome newspaper headline."

"Do you mean to tell me she threatened you?" his mother blurted. "You should have told your father and me. We'll have to notify the police. What if she hurts someone? She needs help!"

"I think her folks have taken her to a psychologist," offered James. *Not that there's any cure for being a vampire.*

"But if she threatened you, James, we need to report it to the police."

"The police are no good for keeping somebody from killing you. You know that. Look at all those poor suckers who get stalked—they get injunctions, they get protective orders, and it doesn't matter a bit in the long run."

"Still—" protested his mother.

James interrupted her. "The only time the cops are any good is for locking people up after they've already killed you."

The line was silent, but James could feel his mother's fear vibrating across the miles.

"I need to get away for a while anyway," James went on. "You know how close I've come to cracking up since Susan died. I've had about all I can take."

"But, James, where *are* you?" she begged.

"We're past Burlington on Highway Forty, at a rest stop. Don't worry, I'm fine."

"How can you be near Burlington when your car is still parked in the driveway?" His mother's voice sounded dangerously calm. James knew she was beginning to wonder if *he* was the one who had cracked up.

He cleared his throat. "Actually, I'm in Rina's car. She's driving me. Have I mentioned Rina Cargiale? She's a new girl at school. She's nice. I've been sort of hanging around with her. I think that's part of the reason Chelsea's freaked out. Maybe this wasn't, uh, the best time to break up with Chelsea." He was afraid his mother, who at times could practically hear his thoughts, might hear a change in his voice when he mentioned Rina. She must know something was going on between them, but of course she could never in a million years guess the truth. "Anyway," he croaked, "Rina's just going to drive me over to Gram's. You know, Chelsea had me blocked in with her car, and I had to get away the best I could, so Rina offered me a lift."

"I don't know, James," his mother said pensively. "I wish you'd let me call the police. I'm not making any promises that I won't. Your father and I have to do what we think is best."

"Fine," said James. "Do whatever you think." It didn't really matter whether his parents called the police, he realized. All that mattered was that he had to keep away from Chelsea. "Now, listen. This part is important, Mom: *Don't tell anybody where I am. It might get back to Chelsea.*"

"I understand."

"I'll call when we got to Gram's if it's not too late."

"As if I could sleep a wink until I knew you were safe," she said sharply.

James smiled. "I'll be careful. 'Bye."

Rina sat on a concrete bench outside the plaza, blotting her eyes with a tissue. She was sorry she had let James see how upset she was. She remembered how he had said once that Chelsea was "fun." Rina wanted him to think she was fun, too. And here she was, crying and acting pathetic.

"I hate myself," she muttered. A branch dripped water on her head, but she didn't bother to move. It was as if the tree were weeping for her.

She should be happy. James liked her better than Chelsea now. But somehow that wasn't enough. She didn't want to be his vampire sidekick or his pretend girlfriend. She wanted something real and warm to grow between them. Something human. Something wonderful. It seemed to hover just out of her reach.

A short dark man with a beaked nose walked past her. At the sight of him, Rina trembled.

"Nick!" she exclaimed, and the man spun around. Hair threaded with gray. High arched brows. Framed luminous brown eyes. Standing not four feet away, he looked Rina straight in the eye. She saw him blink rapidly, then gulp, and a smile froze on his face.

"I'm sorry," he muttered. "But you must have me confused with someone else."

Her sharp eyes took in the slight redness on one nostril, as if a pimple were starting there. Faint creases showed at the corners of his dark eyes. She gazed at him in amazement. "Niklas Grigorescu!" she cried. "What's happened to you?"

A little boy in a windbreaker ran up and grabbed the man's hand. The dark child stared at Rina. "Who's she, Daddy?" The child, who must have been about five, spoke in a flat American accent, not at all like the cultivated and faintly foreign sound of his father's voice.

Rina was so staggered, she couldn't speak. She stared at the little boy.

"Please excuse us," said the dark man. "We're in a hurry." He jerked the child along the gleaming sidewalk.

"Hey!" protested the little boy.

Rina watched them hurry through the mist and climb into a burgundy Chevrolet. At first she was too stunned to move. But the sound of the car's motor made her leap to her feet and run after them. She saw that a woman was sitting in the passenger seat and another child was in the backseat.

The car sped away with a puff of white exhaust, but not before Rina had read the license plate. She pulled a dollar bill from her wallet and jotted the number on it. Not that she expected to forget it.

James had stepped out from the overhang and stood under the light, shivering.

"James!" she cried. "Something has happened!"

He blanched. "Is it Chelsea?"

"No! No!" Rina grabbed his hand and pulled him to the car. It hurt her to see his face pale with cold, and she wanted to get him out of the chill damp and turn on the car's heater. He had left his house too suddenly to grab a jacket, and she had to control the almost overwhelming impulse to offer him hers.

"What, then?" he said. "Give me the keys, Rina. I'll drive."

She handed him the keys and settled meekly into the passenger seat. Excitement sizzled under her skin until she felt she would explode.

The big car sped onto the highway.

"You scared me to death," James complained. "Here I was talking to my mother about Chelsea and you say, 'Something has happened.' I figured you were going to break it to me that coming through phone lines was another little trick vampires could pull off."

"No! James, listen!" Rina took a deep breath. "I just ran into somebody I used to know."

James eyed her warily. "Who?"

"His name is Nick. He was a friend of Vlad's."

A groan escaped James. "Oh, no! We're already up to our ears in vampires. You think he's on his way to meet up with Vlad?"

"I'm sure he's not."

"How can you be sure of anything?" James asked dolefully.

"Because he's real! Nick has turned into a human being! He's gotten older! He's with a woman and two little boys!"

James exhaled a long breath. "Calm down, Rina."

"I can't!" Rina yelped. "This is wonderful!" Her voice broke. "It's incredible! Don't you see? Nick must know how to become human! This is what I've been hoping for!"

She felt James's hand enfold hers. His eyes stayed on the road ahead, but she could see that they were unnaturally bright with emotion. "I want it for you, too, Rina," he said huskily. "You know I do."

She withdrew her hand from his. "You don't believe me," she said.

"I believe you saw somebody who looked like Nick," he said.

"It *was* Nick!" she pleaded. "It *was!*"

James glanced at her. "Rina, you remember how sad I was when my sister died? Listen, I used to think I saw her. I'd hear a noise and I'd spin around, sure it was her. I wanted it so much that I almost made myself believe it."

"This isn't like that." Rina lifted her chin. "I memorized his license number. I wrote it down, too."

They drove in silence for several minutes.

"Why don't you believe me?" she wailed.

He squeezed her hand.

"Don't humor me!" she sobbed. "This is important to me!"

"Rina, the dead don't come back to life. They just don't."

"I'm not really dead," she whispered.

James didn't speak for a while. Finally he said, "You're right, Rina. I don't know anymore what's possible and what's not. I hope you can find the guy."

Rina clenched her fists. "I've got to."

9

It was midnight when James turned the car onto the long, unpaved driveway that led to his grandmother's house. The car's headlights struck the fence that lined either side of the roadway. At the end stood a frame house, brightly lit with floodlights shining from beside its door into the white mist.

"That's the stable over there." James pointed to a barnlike structure swimming in the mist. "Do you ride?"

Rina gulped. "No. I can't."

"I could teach you."

She shook her head miserably. "I really can't, James. No horse will let a vampire near it. All I'd have to do is go close to the stable and they'd be kicking against their stalls."

"Too bad." James's voice was even and expressionless, but Rina would have felt better if he'd been less controlled. She had the feeling he was bottled up and ready to explode.

The car bumped over uneven ground and stopped just short of the back door.

"I hope your grandmother likes me," said Rina.

"She'll like you." James handed her the car keys, and Rina tucked them into her pocket.

The door of the house opened as they got out, and a tall woman stood before them. "James! Come in, come in!" she called.

Nancy Fenner, James's grandmother, had a crop of wiry hair that must have once been blond but was now some light, indeterminate color. Khaki pants and a flannel shirt hung on her bony frame. On her feet were blue nylon bedroom slippers.

James embraced her. "I'm glad we didn't wake you up, Gram."

"How could you wake me up? I've been waiting for you. Nina called me and told me about Chelsea. What a terrible thing! I never dreamed she was so unstable."

"Gram, this is Rina," James said, introducing the two.

The older woman smiled and enfolded Rina. Rina was drawn so close that her nose pressed against the buttons of the old flannel shirt. "You're like ice, child!" Mrs. Fenner exclaimed. "Get inside, you two." She shooed them indoors.

Rina wished James's grandmother had not hugged her. As she darted into the warm kitchen, she was morbidly conscious of how cold she had become. It had been a long time since she had fed, but the thought of searching for human prey sickened her. What was going to become of her, she wondered miserably, if she had lost her will to feed?

"Hot cocoa will fix you up!" Mrs. Fenner busied herself at the kitchen stove.

James pulled out a chair for Rina at the kitchen table, and then slid into one across from her. He smiled. "My grandmother has a secret recipe."

"No secret to it," Mrs. Fenner said. "I triple the cocoa and leave out most of the sugar. That's the way the Aztecs took their cocoa; a good jolt of caffeine."

"Sugar is for sissies," explained James.

James's grandmother pushed two steaming mugs in front of them. "This will do the trick."

Rina cradled the mug in her cool palms and took a deep breath. Nothing would warm her but hot, rich blood.

"At least it'll get your attention," said James, his eyes meeting Rina's in a quick look of sympathy.

"This is terrible driving weather—nothing but drizzle and fog," Mrs. Fenner said, sitting down at the table. "The road hasn't had a chance to dry off all day. I'm just glad you kids arrived in one piece."

Rina could not think of anything but her urgent need to find Nick Grigorescu. "I wonder if there's a way to trace a person's license plate," she asked abruptly.

Mrs. Fenner paled. "You kids didn't get hit!"

"No. It's just that I thought I saw someone I knew." Rina stared down at her hands self-consciously. "And I wondered if there was any way to trace him."

"Seems like a lot of trouble to go to," said Mrs. Fenner dubiously. "You mean, you just saw this person in a car along the road?"

"It was when we were pulling out of a rest stop near here," said Rina. "The car had a parking decal for Heritage Hospital and a bumper sticker that read, 'I have a terrific kid at Cooper's Elementary.'"

Mrs. Fenner gave her a sharp look. "Cooper's Elementary isn't ten minutes away from here."

James slid his chair back suddenly. "We'd better be getting on to bed, Gram. We're keeping you up."

"You aren't keeping me up. As if I could sleep after what your mother told me!" she snorted. "How did you ever get mixed up with such a crazy girl as Chelsea, James?"

"I don't know, Gram." James shrugged uncomfortably. "Had I better go get your suitcase, Rina?"

Rina jumped up. "No, let me do it. Please."

When she came back, James and his grandmother were talking quietly, and Rina felt the pain of being an outsider.

Mrs. Fenner looked up at her and smiled. "Well, you kids will be okay out here with me. Do you ride, Rina?"

"No!" Rina and James both spoke at once.

"We'll have to teach you, won't we?" Mrs. Fenner began clearing away the cups.

"Rina's afraid of horses," said James.

"We can put her on Boss," his grandmother said comfortably. "She's as broad as a bed and hasn't taken any interest in anything but her oats for ten years. It's like sitting in an easy chair, Rina."

Rina shot James a frightened glance.

"We've got enough on our plate right now, Gram, without tackling Rina's phobias." James leaped up. "Let me show you where to put your things, Rina."

Rina followed him down a long, dark hall. He opened a door to show a pine-paneled room. Ruffled cotton curtains with a sprigged flower design covered the windows, and a matching bedspread covered the bed.

"Let's see if the bed is made up." James pulled back the bedspread. "Sheets and pillowcases, check," he said. "We're in business." He met Rina's gaze. "Gram is going to think it's pretty strange if the sheets aren't wrinkled, so at least get on the bed and roll around some, okay?"

Rina nodded unhappily. "I'm afraid your grandmother doesn't like me."

"She likes you. It's just that she knows something fishy is going on." James took a deep breath. "But she'll never guess the truth about it, so what are we worried about?"

"I don't know," said Rina miserably. "Oh, what's wrong with me? I thought if we ran away together, I'd be so happy."

James took her hands in his and gazed at her with a troubled expression. "You are cold—I mean, *really* cold. No wonder Gram said you were like ice."

Rina gulped. "I get that way sometimes." She glanced around the bedroom. The central heat vent was by the bed and made a slight rattling sound.

James frowned. "Look, I've got to go back to the kitchen. I've got to call Mom, and Gram wants to pin me down for a heart-to-heart as soon as I get you settled. She wants to know everything about Chelsea. After she's finished pumping me about Chelsea she'll start working on you."

"What are you going to tell her about me?" Rina asked anxiously.

He grinned. "As little as possible. Officially," he said, "you and me are friends. She isn't going to believe it, but that's my story, and I'm sticking to it."

"But aren't we friends?"

"Well, sure we're friends. But not *just* friends."

"I'm not your girlfriend, though," Rina said regretfully. "Not really."

"Nope." James smiled at her wryly. "We don't have to worry about that stuff right now, Rina. We're here. They didn't catch up with us. That's enough, isn't it?" He slipped out and quietly closed the door after him.

No, she thought, *that is* not *enough*. Rina fell onto the bed and lay there, feeling suffused with loneliness. She heard the low murmur of voices in the kitchen, James and his grandmother talking. The two of them were related—that meant they had the same blood in their veins. Blood. The word rang in her mind as she rolled and twisted on the sheets, but her body was so close to weightless that it scarcely wrinkled them at all. It seemed to her she felt even lighter than was usual—like a piece of fluff drifting in a cold wind. She wadded the top sheet, clutching handfuls of it in her fists to make wrinkles.

James and his grandmother talked for a long time. At last Rina heard footfalls going down the hall. They were going to bed. The room got darker, and she realized that someone had turned off the outside floodlights.

Rina clutched her temples. There was something she ought to be doing, but she couldn't remember what it was. The cold in her arms and legs had begun to seep into her brain, and she wasn't sure she was thinking straight. She could feel herself going wispy and vague, and fear made her rigid. All she could think about was that she was hungry. Blood. She squeezed her eyes closed and tried to focus her mind. Something important kept slipping just out of her consciousness. Nick. Nicky. Something about him.

The bedroom door opened, showing a faint rectangle of light. Rina slid lightly off the bed at once, her heart racing. Her fangs slipped out of their sheaths.

"It's only me," whispered James.

In the dark he looked insubstantial and wraith-like—the way he had when she first caught a glimpse of him one night in the cemetery—but he drew close to her, and she felt his warmth. He took her cold hands in his. "Rina, are you okay?"

She gulped. "Sure."

"No, you're not. You're cold. You haven't felt this cold before."

Rina knew that cold was rolling off her body. When she was this way, it was as if she sucked the heat from the atmosphere around her. She had seen people shiver as she approached. "I forgot to feed," she admitted.

A stunned silence lay between them for a moment.

Rina spoke quickly. "I stole some blood from the blood bank. I thought that would keep me alive. But it wasn't the same, somehow. It didn't work."

"Jeez, Rina. I didn't know that you *had* to have the stuff."

"I don't want to feed anymore, James." She gulped. "Don't you see? I've got to become human. Soon. Or something awful may happen to me."

"How much time do you have left?" James asked.

"I don't know." In the distance a horse whinnied. "I don't even know what will happen if I don't feed. It's just that I can feel myself fading." She choked on a sob. "Maybe it would be better if I disappear."

"Why not bite me?" James asked softly.

Rina took a step backward. Her fangs tingled. "No," she whispered. "I can't."

"I trust you," he said. "Go ahead."

"You shouldn't. I don't trust myself," she said miserably.

"I don't want you to die, Rina." He gripped her hands tightly. Slowly he pulled her toward him until she was so close to him, she could feel the rising and falling of his chest as he breathed.

She felt his warm hand reaching under her hair, pressing her head closer to him. She could feel the heat of his blood pulsing through the great artery at his neck, the hot stream of blood that linked brain to heart. Suddenly she opened her mouth and bit into the soft flesh of his throat. Her mouth was full of blood, and a red haze of excitement shook her. For an instant she felt herself floating on a river of blood, buoyed up by it. But an alarm rang in her mind at once, as if something inside were protesting the terrible feast that nourished her. She pulled away from him abruptly.

When her vision cleared, she was shocked to find James's inert body crumpled under her. "James!" she sobbed, kneeling beside him. "Speak to me!" With a trembling hand she stroked his hair. She touched his chest and realized he was still breathing. He was not dead, then, but unconscious. Rina pressed his limp hand to her cheek, feeling its pulse against her skin. The beat of his heart was strong and steady. She didn't know how long she had drunk his blood; perhaps no more than a second or two.

James jerked his hand out of her grasp, and her heart leaped in relief. He was regaining consciousness.

"Jeez, Rina, that hurt!" he said thickly. "It was like being stabbed. What happened?"

"I bit you," she confessed. "I didn't remember to cast a spell. That's why it hurt. I'm sorry."

"I guess I passed out."

"I feel so *awful!*" she whimpered. "I'm really, really sorry."

"Oh, cut it out," he said irritably. "It's okay. I told you you could do it, didn't I? Why don't you turn on the lights."

Rina turned on the overhead light. James struggled to a sitting position and leaned back, resting his head wearily against the door. His face was so pale she was alarmed, and she knelt beside him. "Don't try to stand up," she whispered.

He pressed his hand to the yellow bruise that had formed around her fang marks. "Ouch."

"Don't you see?" she cried. "I can't go on like this. It wasn't so hard when I slid from moment to moment without thinking, but I've changed since then. Everything's different for me. Now I remember too much what it was like to be really alive, and I can't go on being a vampire. I'd rather be dead."

James struggled to his feet. Rina felt a sick jolt when she realized that his eyes were unfocused.

"Listen," he gasped, "we'll talk about this in the morning, okay? I've got to lie down." Breathing hard, he reached for the doorknob. Rina's heart contracted when she saw that he was leaning against the door. He hesitated at the door a second. "Are you okay now?"

"Yes," she muttered miserably. "But what about you?"

"I'm okay. I just hope when I passed out, my grandmother didn't hear me hit the floor, that's all. Let's get some sleep." He closed his eyes. "Let me rephrase that. *I'll* get some sleep. You can catch up on your knitting or do whatever it is that vampires do in their spare time."

Rina wanted to help him to his room, but she sensed he didn't want her to. So instead she listened anxiously to his halting footsteps in the hallway. At least she did not hear him fall, and a moment later she heard the sound of his bedroom door closing.

She clenched and unclenched her fists in despair. It sickened her to feel the strength and warmth in her hands and to know that she had drained her strength from James. She could never force herself to do it again, she knew. But she was thinking clearly now, and suddenly she remembered what she had to do.

She opened her bedroom door and moved silently down the hall. In the kitchen, a night-light glowed beside the sink, illuminating a plastic bottle of detergent and a paper towel dispenser.

Rina opened cabinets and drawers as quietly as she could until at last she found what she was looking for: a phone book. The slender book had listings from a cluster of six small communities. Rina glanced at the area map on page three, committing it to memory. Then she checked the alphabetical listings. She found no Grigorescu, but under the heading "Woodbine Community," she found a listing for Nick Gregory. Niklas Grigorescu. Nick Gregory. Close enough. She circled it with a red marker with a celebratory flourish.

"Bingo!" she whispered.

Trembling with excitement, she opened the kitchen door and stepped outside into the cold mist. Somewhere behind the clouds a moon was hiding, and a faint radiance illuminated the night. She glanced around the misty yard, looking past her parked car. White fences that vanished into the haze gleamed on either side of the dirt driveway, which showed a dun color, lighter than the grass that hemmed it on either side.

Rina let herself grow misty to blend with the vaporous air. Then she slipped to the back of the house. She passed by the heat pump, which shuddered, then settled into a steady hum. A big Jeep Cherokee was parked in back, and Rina ran wispy fingers along its moisture-frosted hood. She glanced uneasily toward the stable looming out of the mist.

A broad oak grew twenty yards beyond the house, and she moved toward it and stepped into its shadow. She focused her energy until she could feel it burning painfully hot, like a throbbing knot where her heart was. Then she fell to her hands and knees and watched as her limbs became spindly and fragile. Her feet hardened, growing tight and compact until she could pound the bare ground with a slender hoof. Her heart was beating faster now, and her nose felt cold. She sniffed curiously at the air. Her buff-colored fur gleamed palely in the shadows.

A doe bounded out from under the tree and ran lightly across the grass. As the deer sprang past the stable that loomed large and light in the mist, the sound of screaming horses rent the air. The doe looked at the barnlike structure in alarm, her amber eyes gleaming with intelligence. With a flash of white tail she veered away from it and vaulted off into the woods.

10

A light rain was falling as the deer stood at the intersection of two narrow roads. A sign at the crossroad said WOODBINE COMMUNITY. Water beaded heavily on her thick coat, and her long eyelashes were dark with rain.

She lifted her head to gaze at the sign. "Rina," sighed the doe, being careful not to forget her name. Her white tail flashed in the darkness as she fled down the road in the direction the sign pointed.

Farther along, the woods thinned and disappeared, giving way to farmland on both sides of the road. Ahead she saw the reaching steeple of a small white church. She trotted past houses with mailboxes alongside the road, glancing carefully at each name emblazoned above the numbers. The road widened, and she saw what looked like a small grocery store. In front of it, old-fashioned gas pumps gleamed in the mist.

The deer stopped suddenly and walked carefully up to the store, her delicate hooves clicking on the pavement. She walked close to the large front window and pressed her wet nose against the glass. HARVEST FESTIVAL said a poster board decorated with an orange crayon pumpkin propped up against the glass. Business cards had been taped to the inside of the window, advertising minor services: Scissors sharpened. Golf Clubs repaired. Firewood delivered.

The doe blinked at the cards, then suddenly bounded away. At a ditch by the road, she halted abruptly and stood frozen in stillness as her heart thumped under her ribs. A cat streaked across the road, and its shrill howl split the night. The doe shivered.

Moving more slowly now, she picked her way through the village, pausing at each mailbox to nuzzle it gently and to stare at it with her odd amber eyes. At last she found what she was looking for. GREGORY, the mailbox said on it, 1844 WOODBINE ROAD. The deer glanced at the house beyond the mailbox. It was a modest frame structure set back from the road. She made her way across the mowed yard to a single window that was still brightly lit. She moved close to the window, resting her nose on the windowpane as she peered at a couple sitting in bed. Nick was talking to his wife. The doe cocked her ears, taking in every word.

"I tell you, she recognized me!" cried Nick. "You can imagine how I died a thousand deaths when she called my name! 'Niklas Grigorescu!' she yelled. Just like that."

"But it's been so long! How could you possibly be sure that she recognized you? Besides, I don't see that it matters. She doesn't know where we live."

"She's a vampire, remember? She has powers." Nick laughed bitterly. "If Roger keeps on the way he's going, he may turn me back into a vampire, too."

"He wouldn't do that."

"Are you sure? He's gotten so eccentric! So bitter! Sitting in that big house over there, trying out magic spells nonstop, would be enough to drive anybody crazy."

"Go to sleep, Nick. Talking about it isn't going to solve anything. Remember, this girl may never show up. Even if she does, Roger wouldn't blame you."

"Well, he's not going to make her human," says Nick, turning out the light. "He said he wasn't going to do that anymore."

His wife rolled over. "I guess he doesn't like the way we've turned out."

"What'd he want? We pay our taxes and raise our kids. What more can he expect?"

"He's always been strange, and it's gotten worse. But what's the use of worrying ourselves sick over something that might not even happen? It's four A.M., and we've got to get up and go to work tomorrow!"

The room was plunged into darkness, and the voices fell to low murmurs. The doe did not strain her ears any longer to try to make out what they were saying. She had heard enough. "Roger," they had said, the "big house over there." It sounded as if the magician lived right in the community, per-haps near where she was standing.

The deer lifted her head and looked around. A nearby house stood at the beginning of a rise in the land, set a bit apart as if it fancied itself the aristo-crat of the village. It was older than the other houses and had grander pretensions. Roger's house? The deer bolted toward it.

Moments later she stood on the path leading to its front porch. Potted chrysanthemums stood on either side of the porch steps. Seeing a moving shadow on the porch and hearing a rusty squeak, the doe shied a little. She stood trembling, and saw a porch swing move in the breeze.

The deer could smell the scent of herbs hung to dry on the porch. A magician's house, to be sure. A blast of snoring shook the windows of an upstairs bedroom. If she woke the eccentric magician now, she realized, he would certainly not be in a good mood. It would be better to return later.

The deer bent her head and sniffed curiously at the path. She smelled the track of an old and sick animal with something sour clinging to the spoor. A flame of fear flickered in her brain. What if the old magician were near death? He might die be-fore he returned her back into a human being.

A dog yipped. The doe's heart thudded in panic, and she bounded off.

On a road some miles away, Chelsea gripped the steering wheel tightly, and her car skidded around a hairpin curve. "I love being a vampire," she said. "No seat belts, no worries, and I can go as fast as I want."

Vlad popped a small pill into his mouth and clutched his stomach.

"That motion sickness is all in your mind," Chelsea said, giving him a brief glance. "You shouldn't let it get to you the way you do."

"I wish a police officer would stop us and give us a ticket," said Vlad dourly.

"Bite your tongue."

He glanced at her and made a face. "I'd much rather bite a cop."

"Got the munchies, huh?" Chelsea grinned. "Not to worry. We'll be there pretty soon. You can have the grandmother. I want James all to myself."

Vlad leaned his head back and groaned. "Slow down, Chelsea! I implore you!"

"They've just got to be at James's grandmother's." Chelsea's eyes narrowed. "James is not the type to take off for New York or New Orleans. He'd want to go someplace where his parents wouldn't worry about him. And that means his grandmother's."

"Slow down!" pleaded Vlad.

A deer leaped in front of them, and a thud shook the car. Chelsea saw the deer's frightened amber eyes when it hit the windshield. The tires squealed as the car skidded to a stop.

Chelsea opened the car door and jumped out. "It's a lucky thing we didn't wreck." She frowned. The car lay sideways across the lane, and fog seemed to be closing in on them. Chelsea poked the deer's body with the toe of her shoe. "You'd better get this thing out of the way for me," she yelled to Vlad.

Vlad groaned and got out of the car. "What do you expect when you drive like a maniac?" He bent and grabbed the deer's legs and pulled it to the side of the road. Weeds stirred in the mist as he pulled the body off into the undergrowth.

Returning to the car, he wiped his palms against his jeans. "You realize," he said, "that if you hadn't been going too fast, we wouldn't have struck that creature."

"Don't be stupid. It could have happened to anybody. The deer came out of nowhere. Besides, it's a break for us, as it turns out. Lookee there." Chelsea pointed. The car's headlights shone directly on a wooden sign that said FENNER STABLES. "If I hadn't hit the deer, I might have driven right past it."

She bent to check the bumper for damage, then got back in the car and started the motor. She turned in at once at the dirt road that led to the Fenner property and switched off her headlights.

Vlad blinked. "What are you doing?"

"I don't want anybody in the house to know we're coming. Headlights would announce us."

"Do you have to bump so much?" Vlad grumbled.

"I didn't make this crummy road," retorted Chelsea.

"Well, go slow."

"If I slow down anymore, we'll just rock instead of bump," she said, "and you'll be just as sick."

Vlad unrolled the window and stuck his head out. Rain was running in streams down the windshield, and Chelsea switched on the windshield wipers.

"Vlad, what color were that deer's eyes?" she asked.

"What?"

"Would you get back in the car so you can hear what I'm saying?" she snapped.

"I need fresh air," he complained.

"Didn't you hear me?" snarled Chelsea. "I asked you what color that deer's eyes were."

He smoothed rainwater out of his hair with his hands. "I don't know. Whatever color deer's eyes usually are. Brown, maybe? I didn't notice."

"I have this feeling," Chelsea said, her eyes narrowing, "that when it hit us . . . I don't know, I had the impression of yellowish eyes."

Vlad stiffened. "Rina! It was Rina!"

Chelsea backed up and turned the car around in the narrow driveway. She turned the headlights back on and sped back the way they had come. "Slow down!" Vlad pleaded. "It's not going to help us if you wreck!"

"We had her!" Chelsea shrieked. "And we let her go! Ooo, I wish I hadn't stopped! If only I had run her over!"

Vlad gazed at her coldly. "Larina belongs to me, and I don't want her run over."

"I only want to make her suffer! Then you can have her. You'll take her prisoner, won't you? You'll suck the will out of her and keep her locked up in your stupid, drafty castle? That would be good. I'd like that."

Vlad smiled. "You are always surprising me, little one. Just when I think you have shown me your nastiest side, an even more revolting one is revealed." He pinned her hand to the steering wheel.

"What are you doing?" she protested.

"Just making sure you don't slap me." He smiled, showing long white fangs. "I remember very well the way you behave when someone displeases you."

Getting back onto the highway, the car came to a jolting halt, and Vlad smacked his head against the dashboard. Chelsea laughed when he got out of the car rubbing his head. The car's headlights shone into the rain and mist, lighting up the white lines marking the edge and center of the highway.

Chelsea jumped out. "It was about here that we hit her, wasn't it? Yes!" She pointed to a dark smear on the pavement. "Where did you drag her body to?"

Vlad walked across the highway and knelt. "In these weeds I think. I wasn't paying close attention at the time, but this would have been the logical place—closest to the point of impact." He frowned. "Unfortunately, the rain has washed away much of the scent."

"Does it smell like Rina?" Chelsea demanded. "Can you tell?"

Vlad shook his head. "It smells like a female deer. I have fed on such creatures once or twice."

Chelsea clenched her fists. "That was no deer. It was Rina! I only saw her for a split second, but I could never forget those weird eyes. Look around!" ordered Chelsea. "She may have managed to crawl into the bushes."

The car's headlights shone blankly into the mist. Chelsea sank to her hands and knees at the road's edge, scrambling along the ground as nimbly as a dog. She sniffed at the damp grass and fallen leaves. A startled rabbit stared at her briefly and then leaped away into the underbrush.

Chelsea collapsed suddenly on the wet ground and wiped her nose on her sleeve. Pine needles had dug themselves into the knees of her sodden jeans, and wet grit and leaves had worked their way into her sneakers. She was soaked and uncomfortable, and for all her frantic efforts, she had found no trace of Rina. Somewhere an owl screeched in the distant darkness.

She heard Vlad thrashing around noisily in the underbrush. "Don't you even care that she got away?" she whined. "I could scream, I'm so mad."

Vlad smiled. "I don't think she will go far. Not when her boyfriend is asleep in that simple peasant dwelling."

Chelsea was stung by his condescending tone. "I'll bet James's grandmother's place is a lot nicer than your stupid old castle."

Vlad stiffened. "Centuries of wealth, refinement, and tradition are in every stone of my family's castle. There is simply no comparison."

"I notice you're not living in the dumb castle now."

"I certainly will return," Vlad said haughtily.

"I'll bet it doesn't have any showers or central heating, either," said Chelsea.

"Naturally not," he said with a sneer. "Nor, as a vampire, do I need such luxuries."

"'Nor, as a vampire, do I need such luxuries,'" Chelsea mimicked. "If you've got so much civilization, why don't you have hot water?"

"My pretensions are flattened by your scathing tongue, as usual." Vlad got in the car and shut the door. But even with the door closed she could hear his mocking laughter, and it set her teeth on edge. No matter what she said to Vlad, he always behaved as if he was one up on her. It was infuriating.

Chelsea was surprised to find how much he still bugged her. She had half a mind to drive off without him—but she knew she might need him to help her deal with Rina. She picked a pine needle fragment out of the wet knee of her jeans and got back in the car.

Chelsea started the engine. She turned the car back around and drove slowly, thinking hard. If the deer was Rina, Chelsea reminded herself, Rina would be stunned and temporarily out of the picture. Then at least for the moment, James must be alone and unprotected. That meant if Chelsea moved quickly, she could make

James into a vampire tonight. She wouldn't even need Vlad.

"Do you smoke?" she asked casually.

"Of course not." He gave her a sharp look. "Why?"

She shrugged. "Just wondering."

Their eyes met briefly, and Chelsea had the uneasy feeling that he was reading her mind. "My dear little cabbage leaf," he purred, "don't even think it."

"Think what?" asked Chelsea, wide-eyed.

"Of getting rid of me," he said flatly. It would have been more gratifying if he had seemed a little bit afraid of her. Instead, he rapidly lost interest in the discussion. He opened a map on his lap and frowned at it. "How far are we, would you say, from Woodbine Community?"

"You're the one who's got the map."

Vlad squinted at the map's legend. "Turn on the light," he said.

"Not a chance," said Chelsea as the car bumped back onto the dirt road. "I already told you that I don't want them to see us coming. What's the big deal about this Woodgreen place?"

"Wood*bine*," Vlad corrected. He folded the map and stuffed it back in the glove compartment. "I have an appointment there tomorrow night. The place looks close by. Perhaps only three or five miles away. I can walk or fly if necessary."

"Why would you have an appointment in a little town near here?" Chelsea asked irritably.

"You may sneer at the castle of my ancestors," Vlad said with a smile, "but its fame has reached even to these remote communities. A magician in Woodbine has begged an interview with me."

"A magician!" snorted Chelsea. "I don't believe in magic."

Vlad glanced at her. "You were hatched from an egg, perhaps?"

His superior-sounding laughter rang in Chelsea's ears, and she gritted her teeth.

In the dark woods, an injured deer dragged herself painfully along, leaving a trail of blood on the fallen pine needles and decaying leaves. She could feel blood crusting at the back of her head, matting her fur. She was overcome by dizziness, and her head hurt dreadfully. What was her name, she wondered? It seemed terribly important to remember, but her head hurt too much. Folding her legs under her, she shivered and let her head droop until blackness engulfed her.

11

⟨◆⟩

James was not sure what woke him up. He had the vague sensation that he had heard the horses. But when he awakened, he listened and heard nothing unusual. He lay motionless and weak, as if anesthetized. The unaccustomed feel of his grandfather's big pajamas with the drawstring at the waist made him feel as if he were in disguise. Somehow he wasn't quite himself.

Then he remembered that he had let Rina drink his blood, and uneasiness made his flesh creep. He hated to admit even to himself what he had done. He had been so frightened for her that he had been willing to let her feed on him to bring life back into her chilled flesh.

He threw back the covers and let the soles of his feet touch the floor. It struck him that he had behaved stupidly—much as he cared for Rina. What did he really know about the dark forces that drove her? He hadn't even realized until tonight that she needed human blood to survive.

He stood up and had to catch hold of the bedpost when dizziness hit him. He had seen donors during blood drives at the mall drinking soft drinks and eating cookies and doughnuts. Getting something out of the fridge was not, he decided, a bad idea. He was probably dehydrated. Suddenly he realized that he hadn't had a bite to eat since lunch.

When he got to the kitchen, he glanced out the window and saw Rina's car standing ghostly in the mist. He let the curtain fall closed and poured himself a tall glass of orange juice. The sides of the glass frosted over as he slid a package of doughnuts off the top of the fridge and took out a couple. They felt stiff, a bit stale, but he ate them anyway.

James gulped the juice down quickly, then made himself a cheese sandwich. Snacking in the middle of the night reminded him of Trip, whose raids on his family's refrigerator were legendary, and he felt tears sting his eyes. *Don't look back*, he told himself. *It's over. It can't be helped.*

He headed back to his bedroom, but something made him stop outside Rina's room. Light shone through a crack under the door, but though he listened intently, he heard only silence. Impulsively, he pushed the door open. The room was empty. He was rocked with surprise. Where could she be?

Uneasily, he remembered his vague impression that he had heard the horses. Surely Rina would not have gone to the stable after she herself had told him that horses were terrified of her!

He went to his room and quickly dressed. The hair

on the back of his neck prickled with uneasiness as he pulled on one of his grandfather's jackets from the closet. Odd how no one could bear to clean out the closets after someone died. His grandfather, Susan— their clothes still hung in their rooms as if they were expected back. But perhaps it wasn't so odd after all. The border between life and death seemed more permeable to him now than it once had.

Tiptoeing past his grandmother's room, he slipped out the back door. As soon as he stepped into the chill night air, he could tell the horses were restless. He heard movement, the sound of stomping hooves, and a low nervous whinnying. James's sneakers made a soft, sucking sound on the soggy ground as he walked toward the stable. His toes stiffened with cold. He brushed his wet hair out of his eyes.

When he reached the stable, he lifted the latch and slipped inside. The darkness was rich with the smell of horses and hay. He flicked on the single bulb that hung over the equipment rack, and bridles and saddles leaped into view.

"Rina?" he said quietly.

James's favorite horse, Silky, heard his familiar voice and stuck her nose out of her stall. She lifted her lip and whinnied at him. He walked over to her and scratched her nose gently, letting her hot breath blow damply in his face. "Good girl. Good Silky. You haven't seen a runaway vampire around anywhere, have you?" As if she understood him, she snorted and shied away. "Just kidding," James added.

He glanced around but saw no sign of Rina. Then he froze. He had become conscious of a low vibration growing louder—and recognized the sound of a car's engine. It was getting closer. He cracked the door and peered outside, but he could make out no headlights. The drive was so aligned with the stable that a car coming down that road usually flashed its headlights momentarily into the hayloft. This car must be driving without lights. James glanced uneasily at the light he had turned on. It was shielded by the overhanging haylofts, but he knew it would be seen if anyone looked toward the stable. The large open window over the doors of the stable where hay was loaded into the loft would be perceptibly lighter to anyone who knew what the stable usually looked like at night.

James hoisted a saddle off the wall. Leaving it on the saddle block, he unlatched Silky's stall. Nervous, the big horse shied a little as he slipped on the bridle. He patted her neck reassuringly and slid on the saddle blanket. Then he quickly saddled her and tightened the girth. Who would be driving tonight without lights except Chelsea? She must have followed him to Gram's. He glanced around the stable, looking for anything he might be able to use to defend himself. After a moment's hesitation, he tucked a whip into his waistband. Then he remembered his grandmother's old starting pistol. He had no idea whether it was still around, much less whether it still worked, but when he opened the drawer of the worktable, there it lay, next to a box of blanks. James loaded the blanks into the gun. He knew he'd be better off not confronting Chelsea. It would be safer for him to hide or slip away unseen on the bridle path that led into the woods. But what worried him was Gram. She was asleep inside the house, completely unsuspecting.

He decided he'd better mount now because he wasn't sure he could control the mare enough to mount later if she panicked. He hesitated, then switched off the light. It would be a sure giveaway when he opened the door. Once he was up on Silky, he reached out and nudged the door open a few inches.

Rain was falling, but the hidden moon still cast a pearly, diffused light. James saw a car had come to a stop just short of Rina's car. What startled him was that both car doors opened, and two people were getting out. Then he remembered Vlad, and his mouth tightened. What would he do if the vampires broke into the house? It occurred to him that he could fire the starting pistol and create a diversion that would draw them outside. After that, he would have to play it by ear.

Suddenly, to his alarm, the kitchen light flicked on, then the floodlights shone into the night. Both vampires froze in the startling light. The kitchen door opened, and Gram—a pink quilted bathrobe wrapped around her gaunt form—stood blocking their way to the house.

James heard her say something sharp. He supposed she was demanding to know what they were

doing showing up at this hour. Chelsea made a pla-
cating gesture and stepped toward the older
woman. Suddenly, to James's horror, Chelsea
leaped on his grandmother, and the old woman fell.

James nudged the horse with his heels and
urged her toward the house. Her hoofbeats thudded solidly on the soft ground. Silky tossed her
head as James made her trot. Chelsea released his
grandmother and lunged toward him, shrieking
his name. Silky reared, terrified. James thought he
would never forget her scream. The spooked horse
writhed and strained to get back to the stable.
James was too busy trying to stay in the saddle to
think of anything else, but when at last he glanced
over his shoulder, he saw that Chelsea was standing stock-still. James drew the starting pistol,
aimed it at her, and fired. Chelsea instinctively hit
the dirt, but the other vampire ran and leaped at
him. James saw the vampire's face clearly as he
flew through the air: his unearthly beauty, the
strange shimmering eyes, and a jeweled earring
swinging from an earlobe. James instinctively
raised his arm before his face to protect himself.
Then he struck hard at the handsome face below
him with his whip hand and gasped in satisfaction
when the vampire fell back. Looking down, James
saw him crouched on the ground below like an animal. A raw, red welt showed on the bridge of his
nose and an angry gash on one cheek.

This time James didn't try to restrain the frantic
horse when she bolted. He only pulled hard and dug

in his heels to steer her away from the open stable
door. He was afraid the stable would prove a trap.
Silky's hooves thudded heavily on the wet ground as
she veered away and scraped the corner of the stable. James got his foot out of the stirrup just in time
to save it from being crushed against the boards. He
caught his breath sharply when the building's huge
bulk completely blocked his view of the vampires.
Were they coming after him? He couldn't be sure.

Patting Silky's neck encouragingly, he urged
her onto the dark bridle bath that led through the
woods. She was shivering, and flecks of white
foam clung to her coat. He murmured comfort-
ingly into her ear as they walked the dark path.
Trees loomed high over them, almost blocking the
sky, and it was hard for him to see. Fervently,
James hoped Silky didn't step in a rabbit hole and
break a leg. He couldn't stop thinking of Gram's
body lying motionless at the kitchen door. Surely
she couldn't be dead. He refused to believe she was
dead. He hoped he had diverted the vampires' attention and that they were coming after him.

Some minutes later he came to the highway.
From there he could see that the sky was lighter.
Silky's horseshoes clicked metallically on the
pavement. She bent her head and sniffed at the
road, then did a jittery dance. Suddenly she shied.
James hurried her to the other side. He felt dangerously exposed on the open highway and half
expected Chelsea's car to come barreling down
Gram's dirt road toward him.

When he and Silky found the continuation of the bridle path on the other side of the highway, James breathed more easily. He was invisible now, surrounded by the tall pines. He noticed it was easier to make out the tree's shapes against the lighter sky.

He hoped that if Rina came back to the house, she would see something had gone wrong and would sheer off. He hated to think she might walk smack into Chelsea and Vlad, but he had no way to warn her. And his first priority was to get help for Gram.

Rain from the trees dripped steadily and softly onto the fallen pine needles as the horse made its way along the narrow path. James knew he would find a pay phone at the nearby community of Woodbine, and he headed in that direction.

Without warning, the horse reared. Caught by surprise, James found himself lying stupidly on the ground as his horse galloped ahead. He leaped to his feet and ran after her. She stopped short up the path and when he caught up with her, the whites of her eyes showed in the faint morning light as she pawed at the ground. She skittered away from him, but at last he succeeded in grabbing the reins and calming her.

"What's wrong, Silky?" he murmured. "Hey, girl, calm down. Did you see a snake?" James looked back at the stretch of trail they had passed. He saw nothing there. Only the gentle motion of the leaves as raindrops struck.

But the horse's panic reminded him that the vampires could be close behind him. He'd better keep moving—and as quietly as possible. One good thing was that though Chelsea had visited his grandmother's with him once in the summer, they had done a lot of swimming and had not ridden the bridle path. She probably didn't even know where it was.

The phone at Woodbine was a good three miles by car, but the bridle path was a more direct route, and before long James found himself coming out of the woods near the store. The dim first light of dawn touched its gas pumps and illumined the plastic phone box affixed to a pole by the road. James rode over to it, tied Silky to the pole, and dialed 911.

12

"Don't just stand there!" screamed Chelsea. "Go after him!"

Vlad clutched a hand to the gash on his cheek. "*You* run after him. See how you like being hit in the face and having a thousand-pound beast rear over your head, trying to hammer you with its iron-shod hooves."

"You aren't telling me you're afraid of James!" Chelsea said with a sneer.

Vlad neatly stepped over Nancy Fenner's body and flicked a light on in the kitchen. "It's Rina I'm after," he called over his shoulder, his voice sounding hollow now that he was indoors. "I don't care about him."

Chelsea knelt to touch the ground, feeling the imprint of the horse's hooves in the soft earth. The smell of the animal's terror clung to the mud. Moving on all fours, she followed the horse's trail. When she reached the stable, where the soft ground was heavily trod, the walls of the stable shook with the panicked shrieks of the beasts inside. Chelsea shivered and moved away from the stable. She could feel the ground vibrate from the drumming of hooves.

She bent low, sniffing closely at the ground and frowning. Drizzle was falling, and she was confused by a mixture of scents. She let herself go a little misty as she wandered into the nearby woods. If she came upon James, she knew she could easily creep up on him without his realizing it. Right now she was barely visible. Her mouth watered at the thought. She was certain he was in the woods somewhere. Something told her that he would have instinctively sought cover among the trees. But rain dripped monotonously on the forest floor and washed all scent from the air.

Disappointed in her search, she returned at last to the edge of the woods and stooped on the ground between the stable and the trees, hoping to pick up the trail there and then follow it into the woods. But the ground had been hammered hard beyond the stable—other horses had passed this way, and the ground was slick with manure. Chelsea couldn't sort out the smell of James's horse from the others. *James*, she thought urgently. Longing for him was sharp, like a pain in her heart. She felt vaguely aggrieved at him for being so determined to escape her. Why couldn't he cooperate? When she had envisioned catching up with him, she had always pictured him sleeping helplessly, his beautiful throat exposed. Remembering that dream now, she felt her fangs stir as her human form returned. She had never thought she would have to drag him off a rearing horse while he shot at her face with a pistol. Why did he have to be so difficult!

Suddenly she lifted her head and listened. She could barely hear Vlad's voice because the horses were making such a terrific racket, but she thought he was calling her name. It was hard to believe she had once loved horses. They were stupid, she now realized, and their shrieking, hysterical voices set her teeth on edge. Chelsea stood up and strode toward the house, her sneakers leaving shallow prints on the soft ground.

Nearing the house, she could see the pink of James's grandmother's bathrobe outstretched under the floodlights. When she drew closer, she saw that the old lady's face was a ghostly white. One of her slippers had fallen off, and her bare foot stuck straight up, showing yellowish toenails. Unconcerned, Chelsea stepped over her body and into the kitchen. "What were you yelling about?" she demanded.

"I think I know now where we'll find James and Rina," said Vlad. He had both hands on the kitchen table, and Chelsea saw that he was leaning over an open phone book. Curious, she came up beside him and saw that a name on one page had been circled in ink.

Vlad's eyes narrowed. "Rina has gone to visit an old friend."

Chelsea picked up the phone book and examined the circled name. "Nick Gregory? He's some-body Rina used to know?"

"Yes." Vlad drew out the final consonant so that he sounded like a snake hissing. "I need to pay our old friend Nick a visit."

Chelsea spun around abruptly to face the open kitchen door. "Did you hear that?"

Vlad froze. "What?" he whispered. "What did you hear?"

"It's a siren." Chelsea's face crumpled in disap-pointment. "James must have called the cops. We're going to have to get out of here." She clenched her fists. "Why is he running from me? Nothing is going right. I can't even turn into a mist when I really really need to. Like now!"

Vlad grinned, his fine white teeth flashing. "That's because it's quite impossible to empty one's mind and plan an escape at the same time. Inconvenient but true." His smile disappeared. "And unfortunately, I can hear dawn approaching."

"It's still dark," protested Chelsea.

"Yes, but the sun is even now hammering away at the horizon. Don't you feel the power leaking out of you?"

The wailing klaxon hurt Chelsea's ears. She peered out the kitchen window and saw a line of flashing red lights in the mist. "It's an ambulance," she said bleakly. "They're here."

Vlad glanced toward the dark hallway. "Come on. We can get out the back way."

"But I can't leave my car!" protested Chelsea.

Vlad jerked her arm. "Stupid one! We can always return for the car. But for now, we must escape."

The fear in Chelsea's heart told her that Vlad was right. The two vampires ran through the dark house and slipped out the back door.

"Rina!" Vlad whispered ecstatically, as soon as they stepped into the wet mist. "She has been here! I know it!"

Chelsea stiffened. "She's here? Now?"

Vlad stooped down and groped at the ground with his fingers. "Not now. But the scent is fresh. They are nearby, my sweet." He smiled wolfishly. "And now that we know where they are going, we will catch up with them!"

After calling 911, James untied his horse and glanced around at the sleeping village, its houses stained yellow by the first rays of the sickly dawn. Below him, a cat picked its way around a puddle. On the meandering street that formed the backbone of the village, a lone car drove slowly, stopping at each house only long enough for a gray arm to reach out and toss a rolled newspaper. The scene looked so normal that James found it almost impossible to believe that vampires had attacked his grandmother not three miles away.

He mounted and turned Silky's head toward home. Minutes later, they were back on the bridle path. The horse's ears pricked. She must have realized they were headed back toward the stable, yet her coat twitched uneasily as they made their way along the narrow trail. It was as if she knew something was wrong, and James found himself tensing up.

It seemed strange to him that horses, with their tiny brains and overwhelming instincts, should sense the danger of vampires. And hadn't Rina said that cats were terrified of vampires, too? Maybe it was only intelligence that made it hard for people to recognize the supernatural. James knew that if he let himself be guided not by his mind but by the uncanny prickling at the back of his neck and the shiver in his stomach, it was all too easy to believe that vampires were close at hand.

He thought of the livid gash he had made across Vlad's face with satisfaction as he glanced up at the narrow strip of sky visible through the trees. He reminded himself that daylight would offer its own protection. In daylight, at least, he and the vampires would be on a more equal footing.

A few minutes down the trail, James realized he must be approaching the spot where Silky had thrown him, and he kept alert. This time when she shied, he was ready for her and managed to stay on her back. He let her walk backward for a few yards. In spite of that, she pawed at the ground, shook her mane, and snorted.

"Hold on, girl," James said. "I'll check it out."

Dismounting, he went ahead alone on foot. He prodded the path with his whip in the hope of stirring up snakes. But all his prodding prompted no slithering through the fallen leaves.

James looked around. His skin felt tight, and the hair at the back of his neck stood on end. If not a snake—what then? Suddenly he heard leaves rustle. When he turned his head, he spotted a deer lying just off the path, and his heart gave a thud of relief. Not vampires after all, he realized, but only this harmless deer. And something was wrong with her or she never would have let him get this close.

He saw that the back of her skull was crusted with blood and winced, wishing he had real bullets for the starting gun. He would have liked to put her out of her misery. A truck whooshed in the distance. James knew he must be only some fifty yards or so from the highway. Obviously, the deer had been hit by a car and had somehow managed to drag herself this far.

She lifted her head and looked directly at James, and as he stared into her liquid gold eyes, he felt a sick stirring in the pit of his stomach. "Rina!" he cried.

The doe's mouth opened as if she were about to speak, but instead she shuddered. James heard the leaves overhead rattle and felt an odd vibration in the air. Something strange and uncanny was happening to the doe. Her fur grew sparse, showing the dark flesh underneath. Her legs rounded, and in the dappled and uncertain light James caught a glimpse of blue jeans. He blinked in surprise. The doe's head had fallen between her front legs, and before James's disbelieving eyes the hooves parted and became white fingers. She shook out a mane of black hair and stood up. The back of her head was bloody, but as he watched, the wound was healing. The doe's snout flattened; her wet black nose went pale and took on a delicate human shape between amber eyes. Then he saw that the pale oval he made out in the uncertain light was Rina's face. She combed her fingers impatiently through her hair, shook herself, and stomped the ground in a movement uncomfortably reminiscent of a deer.

"I wish you wouldn't watch when I'm changing," she said. A ray of sun had broken through the pine branches and shot a freckle of sunlight on the forest floor. "Just in time," she sighed. "I wouldn't be able to do it in broad daylight."

Dazed, James passed a hand across his face. No wonder Silky had freaked out, he thought. He was shaking like a leaf himself.

"I feel kind of dizzy," said Rina. Her knees buckled, and she sat down suddenly.

James sank to his knees beside her. "Rina! What happened to you!"

"I forgot my name." She closed her eyes and shivered. "It was awful! Just thinking about it scares me."

"You must have gotten hit by a car," said James. Somehow that sounded all wrong. It had been the doe that was hit by the car. But Rina *was* the doe. He shook his head unhappily. "You must have gotten a concussion."

Her eyes widened. "If you hadn't reminded me of my name, I wouldn't have been able to turn back into myself! Oh, James. I don't think I'll ever have the courage to change form again!"

James struggled to his feet. An unsteady fluttering of his heart made him feel sick. He knew he needed to get away from her so that he could think straight. "L-look, Rina," he stuttered, "I'll be back. But I've got to go check on Gram. Chelsea attacked her, and I've got to make sure she's all right." He hesitated, then added, "I probably ought to warn you that Chelsea brought Vlad with her."

"I know! They hit me with their car!" Rina cried. "I was running to get back to the house. I had something important to tell you. And the car shot out of the fog and hit me. I guess I was stunned for a minute, but I remember hearing Chelsea's voice and then Vlad's." She shivered. "I decided I'd better play dead. My head hurt something awful. Luckily, they didn't realize who I was."

"Hang on. I've got to get my horse."

James walked back along the trail to Silky and laid his hand on her neck. She whinnied and tossed her head. He closed his eyes and tried to breathe steadily. The horse's warmth and her familiar smell comforted him. Finally he said in a voice he scarcely recognized as his own, "Stand back from the bridle path, Rina. You're panicking her."

There was a rustling of leaves behind him. "Don't you want to know what I have to tell you?" she asked. Rina's voice sounded farther away, and he knew she had retreated back into the trees, but he didn't turn to look at her. He just didn't feel up to facing her right now.

"Can you hear me, James?" she called plaintively. "Don't you want to hear my news?"

James heard the faint klaxon of a rescue vehicle. "Later. I'll be back!"

James mounted the horse and forced her against her will to walk ahead. Silky shuddered and her eyes were wild, but he made her go on. At last she passed where Rina had been, and she moved more quickly, her quick hoofbeats sounding soft on the pine-needle trail. James did not look back. His own breath was coming in short gasps.

A few minutes later he reached the highway. Just then a rescue vehicle, red lights blinking, bumped off the dirt road and turned onto the highway. The klaxon gave voice again, and the ambulance careened away, wailing, lights flashing. James knew his grandmother was still alive. The EMTs wouldn't have bothered with the sirens if she was dead.

He turned the horse around and reluctantly guided her back on the bridle path. He found himself shrinking from facing Rina. *Whoever wrote "love conquers all" hadn't seen somebody he cared about being half deer and half human,* he thought unhappily. He only hoped he could keep Rina from knowing just how appalled he was.

He found her sitting cross-legged beside the trail, sucking on a pine needle. Freckles of sunlight fell on her gleaming black hair. He tied Silky at a safe distance from her and walked toward her, his legs heavy and stiff. *What a mess I've gotten myself into,* he thought.

"How's your grandmother?" Rina asked.

James thrust his hands in his pockets. "I hope she's going to be okay. I'll give the hospital a call after a while and check on her."

Rina nodded. "Where are Chelsea and Vlad now, do you think?"

"I don't have a clue." James shook his head. "Can you imagine them attacking an old lady like that, right at her own house?"

Rina's cheeks were stained with sudden color, and James wondered if she, too, had once attacked an old lady. He pushed the thought out of his mind. He would go crazy if he started thinking like that. *Don't look back,* he reminded himself.

"So what's your news?" he made himself say. His voice sounded as if it belonged to someone else.

"I've found Nick, James! He calls himself Nick Gregory now, and he lives right here in one of that bunch of houses they call Woodbine Community." Rina's eyes were sparkling. James found himself thinking how large and liquid they looked. Like the eyes of a deer. "What's more important," she went on excitedly, "is that I've found the magician who knows how to change me into a human!"

James felt his heart battering against his ribs. It sounded crazy, but was there some chance it would work?

"I went to his house last night," said Rina, "but

I didn't think I'd better knock on his door. I was afraid if I woke him up in the middle of the night, it might put him in a real bad mood."

"We've got to talk to him today," James said desperately. He realized he was grabbing at the idea because it seemed like something solid and practical he could do. "Before it gets dark again," he added.

Rina glanced uneasily at his horse. Silky was pawing the ground. "You go ahead, James. I'll meet you down in the village, at the grocery store." She stepped back into the shadows.

James mounted the nervous horse and headed toward the village. The tall, dark trees rose on either side of the narrow trail, hemming him in. *Only one chance*, James thought, his heart pounding wildly.

He rode out of the woods and looked down a slope to the village. It was funny how different the houses looked, once he knew what was going on there. Now he could easily pick out the magician's place; it was a grander-looking house than the others, with a deep, cavernous porch hung with broad wood trim. He could just make out that bunches of weeds were hanging from some kind of line strung above the banisters.

A sorrel mare was grazing in a pasture not far from the magician's house. James rode down to the pasture, unlatched the gate, and shooed Silky in. He felt guilty that he couldn't rub her down after the ride, but luckily she wasn't really hot.

Silky would have to make do for now. He left her grazing and went on foot back to the grocery store.

Rina sat on the curb outside the grocery, hugging her knees. When she spotted him, she leaped up and threw her arms around him. To James's dismay, she felt his back stiffening and pulled away at once.

"You hate me!" she sobbed.

He shook his head. "No, Rina. I just need a little space right now. Can't you understand that?"

"I told you not to watch when I was changing," she said defiantly.

Unerringly, she had put her finger on the problem. It was hard to feel tender toward someone when you only recently watched her molt her fur and turn from a deer into something else. Something—let's face it—not quite human, no matter how breathtakingly beautiful and no matter how nice at heart.

James reached for Rina's cool hand, sorry that he wasn't able to give her what she so obviously wanted from him. "Let's get some breakfast," he said wearily.

The store's lights were on inside, and James could see a young woman standing behind the counter. He pushed the glass door open, glad to be someplace—anyplace—where he was sure of his bearings. Bananas were stacked on the counter by the cashier next to a few bags of onions. A nearby aisle had candy on one side and on the other, a few items each of ordinary household articles: dog food, canned beans, charcoal. The back wall of the store was lined with coolers of soft drinks and milk. James had been in a hundred stores that looked much the same, and the simple familiarity came as a relief. He bought a small carton of milk and a sticky bun wrapped in cellophane. Rina got a colorless, tasteless diet drink. James had never thought before how that kind of drink might have been designed for vampires.

The girl behind the counter had a dusting of freckles and mouse-colored hair that hung down her back. She gazed at them with avid curiosity. "So," she prodded, "are you here on vacation, or are you just visiting?"

"We're visiting," said James. And to spare the girl the trouble of digging for the information, he added, "We're staying with my grandmother, Nancy Fenner."

"Oh, yeah." She nodded. "The lady that runs the stable over by the highway."

James realized that the clerk must know most of her customers by sight, and of course she would notice strangers, just as she had spotted him and Rina. He only just stopped himself from describing Chelsea and Vlad and asking if she had seen them. His nerves were getting to him, he knew. After all, there wasn't any reason to think Chelsea and Vlad would catch up with them here, at this out-of-the-way village.

He took his snack outside, and he and Rina sat down on the curb.

"I'm glad you're going with me to see the magician," said Rina. "I'm scared. What if he should tell me he won't help me?"

"Why would he do that?" James did his best to sound upbeat. "It sounds like he's made other vampires into humans. Why wouldn't he be willing to do it for you?"

"Nick thinks he won't."

"You talked to Nick?" James raised his brows.

"No, not exactly. I overheard him say it to his wife. He said the magician had gotten very strange."

"Well, what do we have to lose by trying?"

"Let's go ask him now!" Rina leaped up.

James glanced at his watch dubiously. "It's pretty early, Rina."

"I can't stand it any longer," she said. "I've got to know."

"Okay." James gulped down the last of the sticky bun, licked his fingers, then stuffed the cellophane wrapping and the empty milk carton into the trash. "Let's go."

Several cars passed them as they walked down the street, and James felt the curious gazes of the villagers on him. He stared back. The cars were packed with kids in quilted jackets and drivers who looked tired. He wondered how many of them had once been vampires.

A pair of swallows dipped and looped over the pasture where he had left Silky. As he and Rina drew close to the big house, he saw that its eaves were decorated with elaborate gingerbread trim on which the carved repeated motifs were the sun, moon, and stars. The roof overhang was deep and cast shadows on the walls of the house. From under pointed gables peered groups of even more fantastic and disturbing carvings: gargoyle faces, grimacing demons, dragons, snakes, and monsters. The effect was strangely disturbing, as if the walls of the house were bulging with supernatural life.

"What's this magician guy's name?" James asked.

"Roger."

"I can't go up there and say 'Hi, Roger,'" said James. "I don't even know him. I can't call him Roger."

"That's not what's bothering you," said Rina in a low voice. "You're afraid, too, aren't you?"

Rina's habit of tuning in to his feelings was a little disconcerting. Sure, he was afraid. Anybody would be. It was only the wildest kind of desperation that was forcing him to think about knocking on the door of a perfect stranger who had a reputation for being eccentric.

James shrugged away his misgivings. "Okay, we'll call him Roger." He took Rina's hand and could feel she was trembling. Their footfalls sounded hollow as they walked together up the front steps of the porch.

A black cat leaped off the porch swing and then plunged off the banister with a loud screech. The abandoned porch swing swayed with a creak. James felt sweat prickling between his shoulder blades. He raised his hand to knock on the door, but suddenly it flew open and he was confronted by a bent old man. His eyes were a blank-looking light blue, and his long white hair stuck out from his head so stiffly that it looked as if he had been trying to tear it out by the roots.

"You rang?" the old man asked in a sarcastic voice.

James and Rina looked at each other, nonplussed.

"Well, what are you waiting for?" asked the old man. "Get to the point. Are you collecting for charity or trying to sell me something? In either case, don't waste your breath. I never give a penny to charity, and I never buy anything."

"We aren't salesmen," said Rina. "Can we come in?"

The old man fixed her with a tight stare. "Oh," he said in a flat voice, "I see. You're one of those. Well, forget it, girlie. I won't help you out."

Rina shot James a glance of dismay. The old man had retreated into his house, but he had left the door cracked. James decided to take that as an invitation. He pushed the door open and stepped in.

He glanced around in astonishment. The room seemed bathed in an odd amber glow, and James realized that the windowpanes were tinted. Dust motes swam in the musty air over a large black circle that had been painted on the bare wood of the floor, enclosing what looked like a star. But around the cleared space defined by the painted circle lay incredibly close-packed clutter. Threadbare oriental carpets were rolled up against bookcases. Shelves groaned under the weight of thick, ancient books with cracked bindings. Atop a bookcase stood a silver candelabra blackened with age, its short black candles dripping wax.

Feather boas, lengths of silk, and bric-a-brac were crowded into the room, and from a corner brooded a stuffed great horned owl. Its large and feathered brown presence peered out from behind long strands of garlic hanging from the ceiling. Cans of beans and a few jars of salsa were piled in a wicker chair, and on the floor beside the chair were heaped carved and brightly painted wooden masks. A ribbon of antique temple bells was draped over a backgammon board, and a huge unabridged dictionary lay open on the floor. Suddenly James sneezed.

"Gesundheit," snapped the magician.

Behind the old man a tall bookcase served as a kind of divider, beyond which James glimpsed another room where a strong light had been clamped to a table.

When James glanced at Rina, he saw that she was staring fixedly at the black circle drawn on the floor.

"Are you expecting a visitor?" she asked.

"What's it to you if I am?" the old man said pettishly. "Live and let live, that's my motto. Mind your own beeswax."

"You know why I've come to see you, don't you?" asked Rina.

"Sure." The old man smiled and showed blackened and missing teeth. "When my tabby took off like that, I got your number right away, kiddo."

"I want to be human," she whispered hoarsely. "I know you have the spell. Give it to me! Please!"

The magician's smile faded. "I don't know what you're talking about. Well, it's been fun, kids. I don't get many visitors these days. But I guess you'd better peddle your encyclopedias elsewhere."

"You made Nick Gregory into a human being!" exclaimed Rina. "Please, help me!"

The magician bent his white head and plucked invisible bits of fluff off his untidy sweater. With a sinking heart, James wondered if the old man was sane.

"Those Gregory children," the magician frowned, "they stomped on my herbs." Suddenly he fixed James with his sharp gaze. "No good deed goes unpunished," he said. "Have you ever heard that?" He waved a bony hand, and James saw he wore a black onyx ring that glimmered with a strange, unsteady light. "I *made* these people, I tell you, and now all they do is bicker, have loud parties, drive noisy cars, and let their children run wild."

"Nobody's perfect," James said.

"Perfect!" snorted the old man. "They're unspeakable!"

"I won't hurt your herb garden," Rina pleaded. "I won't bother you a bit, I promise. Please, give me the spell!"

"You don't know when you're well off, young

lady." The old man looked at Rina slyly. "Human beings die miserably. Now that I'm sick and getting close to death myself, I've decided it's much better to be a vampire."

Rina's eyes widened in horror. She quickly took a step away from him.

The old man cackled. "Don't worry, my pretty. I don't expect you to drink my blood, and I don't expect you to feed me yours, either. I have made other arrangements." He flicked a few specks of lint off his sleeve. "I still have some connections in the vampire community, and I have been fortunate enough to get in touch with an Immortal, a vampire who has become so cold after many centuries of black life that he has actually lost his heart." The magician rubbed his hands together. "I understand that his image doesn't show in a mirror. He is a king of vampires. Meeting him will be a rare honor."

"Do whatever you want with him!" cried Rina. "But first, please, give me a chance to live! I'm only sixteen. All I want is what you've had yourself. One real life. Please, give me the spell! Please!"

"You don't know what you're talking about," snorted the old man. "Where did you get the idea that I had a spell that could change vampires?"

"Nick Gregory," Rina said desperately. "You did it for him. Remember?"

"I think you must be confused, young lady." The old man's eyes wandered to the bookcase behind him. "I have known Nick Gregory for years, and he's always been the same blabbermouth. A completely unsatisfactory person. And that goes double for his two horrid little boys. I think you'd better leave."

James grabbed Roger by the shoulders. "We'll leave," he shook the old man, "as soon as you give us the spell!" He could feel angry blood pounding in his ears.

"I have a heart condition!" the magician protested weakly. "If you aren't careful, you may kill me."

The sour smell of the man's clothes was in James's nostrils, and he loosened his grip, suddenly feeling sick. He closed his eyes as he pulled away, appalled that he had laid hands on a frail old man.

"Please!" begged Rina. To James's horror she sank to her knees and plucked beseechingly at the magician's loose pants legs. James wanted to grab her hand and run, but he knew he couldn't. It was her own life she was pleading for. He clenched his fists and said nothing.

The old man kicked at her, but catching James's angry look, he backed away hastily. "You kids are making me nervous. Go away. I'm just a sick old man, and I can't help you."

Rina sobbed as she stood up. "Haven't you ever cared about anybody?"

"Not lately." The old man hugged himself. "Get out! This is private property! I could have you charged with trespassing." He glanced at James. "Not to mention assault and battery."

James couldn't take it anymore. If Rina wanted

to stay and beg the wicked old man for mercy while he kicked at her, she was going to have to do it by herself. He couldn't stand here and watch.

He turned on his heel and walked out the door. As he hesitated on the porch, blinking in the light and wondering what to do next, the door flew open and Rina came hurtling out. Obviously the old creep had pushed her. The door slammed shut behind her. James slid his arm around her waist and felt her sag helplessly against him. She seemed pathetically small.

"Oh, James," she sobbed softly. "What am I going to do?"

James gave her a squeeze. "He's got the spell, all right."

"But he won't give it to us!"

James hesitated. "Maybe we could steal it."

"We don't even know where he put it. He's a very powerful magician, James. How can we possibly fool him?"

A fresh breeze was blowing, and the air smelled wonderful after the fetid staleness of the magician's house. The sky was overcast with dark clouds, but glimmers of brilliant sunshine shone through unexpectedly here and there, and the wet grass sparkled.

"We'll get back in the house somehow," James said. "And then we'll find the spell."

"I know you're just trying to cheer me up," choked Rina.

"No, Rina, don't worry. We'll figure out some

way," said James. *Sure, no problem. Turn one vampire into one human being. Will do.* He smiled a little ruefully. *Well, why not? I've seen stranger things happen.* "The man's got to leave the house sometime," he went on. "We'll park ourselves in sight of the place, and when he does go out, we'll sneak in."

13

James left Rina watching the magician's house and walked to the grocery store. From the pay phone, he called the hospital. He was relieved to learn his grandmother was "resting comfortably" and being treated for shock and blood loss. The hospital receptionist volunteered that Mrs. Fenner would probably be ready to come home before long. With a sinking heart, James realized he was in no hurry for his grandmother to come home. At least in the hospital, he could be sure she was safe.

He bought a bunch of magazines, a pack of playing cards, snacks, and a couple of cheap umbrellas. Then he carried the provisions to where Rina was waiting. They spread out their things on a high wooded point above and to the right of the old man's house. James could see Silky and the sorrel mare grazing in the pasture below, and he also had a clear view of the magician's house from this angle. Behind the house stood a garage, a vegetable patch, and a circular clothesline.

From their vantage point they would be able to see the magician leave, whether he went out the back door or the front.

The hours passed slowly. James had never spent much time reading magazines before, and he was surprised at how empty-minded the articles were. Who cared about celebrities' secrets of weight loss? Only cloudbursts broke the monotony of the day. He and Rina huddled under their almost useless cheap umbrellas and listened to the rain as it wrinkled the covers of the magazines and splashed their jeans, which then steadfastly refused to dry. The air felt wet and close.

James felt as if he had tuned in to Rina's wavelength and could feel all her pain and hope and fear shimmering inside him. But the thoughts that were uppermost in both their minds were too highly charged to talk about.

As the day wore on, the rain let up and the air warmed. James found himself growing drowsy and nodded off. When he woke up, he had a crick in his neck, and his sneakers felt hot where slanting sun was shining on them. He pushed himself up on his elbows and stared at Rina. The leaves of the magazine on her lap stirred in the breeze. In the sunshine her raven hair showed fiery highlights. It fell softly against her pale cheek and trailed against her mouth. James had to control the impulse to brush it away from her face. It was almost impossible to believe that in the first moments of dawn he had watched her change from a deer. Now, in the slanting sunshine of late afternoon, she seemed only a breath away from being human. How could the old magician be so wicked as to not give her a chance to get back the life that had been stolen from her?

Uneasily, James glanced down at the magician's house. Angry black clouds still hung in the sky, and a shadow had fallen over the big house. "I guess I fell asleep, huh?"

Rina smiled at him and nodded. "I love to watch you sleep."

James grinned. "You're pretty hard up for entertainment." He looked down at the magician's house again. "No action yet, huh?"

Just then the front door opened, and the old fellow tottered out. James stiffened. "Rina," he whispered. They stared at the frail figure walking toward the road.

"Sorry," James said flatly. "He's just going to get the mail. False alarm."

The magician leafed through a thick sheaf of circulars and letters as he walked back to the house.

"Who can be writing to him?" Rina asked. "He's a horrible person. He can't have any friends."

"Don't forget all his contacts with the vampires of the world," said James.

Rina lifted James's hand and checked his watch. "How did it get to be so late? Why doesn't he go shopping or something?"

"He never buys anything, remember?"

Rina peered at the silent house that lay below

them and made a face. "If he's got an appointment with a vampire, I guess it's for after dark. It would be."

James glanced at the sky. "Well, it won't be long until dark now."

"I wish we could sneak in there now while everybody in the neighborhood is off at work."

James unwrapped a soggy brownie and surveyed it gloomily. "The old man's got to go out of that house sometime, Rina. We're bound to get a break sooner or later. Nobody's luck is bad all the time."

"Are you sure?" Rina asked.

Shadows were lengthening now, and cars were pulling into driveways. Some kids were kicking a soccer ball around in the churchyard.

Suddenly James stiffened. "Rina, look! I think that's Chelsea's car!"

They gathered armfuls of wet magazines, paper bags, and umbrellas, and scooted back into the trees where they would be hidden. James could feel his heart pounding as he watched Chelsea's car drive up in front of the magician's house.

"Why is Chelsea coming here? It doesn't make sense," Rina said. "I thought he was expecting some famous, ancient vampire."

A boy in tight jeans climbed out of the Mazda on the other side.

"It's Vlad!" Rina laid her hand on James's arm, and he could feel she was trembling. "But Vlad's not a famous vampire! Maybe the magician's got him mixed up with somebody else."

The sight of Vlad sauntering up the path to the

house gave James the creeps. A stray ray of light hit the vampire's jeweled earring and made a star of light against his dark hair. James felt the skin between his shoulder blades tighten and wished he hadn't left his whip down by the pasture gate.

He and Rina stood motionless and watched lights come on inside the house. From a nearby house, a woman's voice called the children in, and they picked up their soccer ball and ran home. One by one the curtains of the magician's house were drawn closed.

Darkness rose from the woods to the sky. James stared at the uncurtained windows at the back of the house, trying to make out what was going on inside. He could see what must be the table in the back room, but that was all. The magician and Vlad must be in front.

Rina clutched James's arm. "I'm afraid that old man is making a mistake to trust Vlad."

"This *is* an honor," said the old man. He glanced at Vlad out of the corner of his eye. "May I say you wear your years well? I didn't expect someone that seemed so, shall I say, hip?" He smiled.

Vlad returned the smile. The old guy still had him mixed up with his grandfather. No problem. Although if family portraits were any guide, he was a lot better-looking than his grandfather. He took off his sunglasses and tucked them in his pocket. Glancing around, he recognized a few books that could have come from the Black Castle's library. The owl, too, was a homelike touch. Most of the taxidermy in the Black Castle had suffered from the damp since the night the peasants had burned the place and did so much damage to the roof, but Vlad had never bothered to throw any of it out.

He glanced around curiously, wondering if the magician ran a flea market on the side. "Nice place you've got here," he commented.

"Thank you," said the magician. He folded his hands.

In other times Vlad would have turned up his nose at the magician. He was a fussy eater and preferred for his prey to be healthy. But tonight he was hungry. He hadn't gotten a chance to feed on the old lady before the rescue vehicle had shown up. It had been an unlucky day all around, he reflected. He had missed out on recognizing the doe as Rina when he had dragged her off the road. Though he had pretended to be unconcerned about the slip, he was still kicking himself. Then Rina's boyfriend had landed a painful blow with that whip right across his nose. The welt—and the gash on his cheek—had disappeared, but the bone was still sore, and Vlad was feeling short-tempered.

"So what's the deal?" he asked. He realized he was starting to sound more and more like Chelsea. It was a tendency he had better nip in the bud.

"The *deal* is that I want you to make me into a vampire!" The old man threw open his arms. His pale blue eyes were ecstatic.

Vlad frowned. "Yeah, but what's in it for me?"

The magician's eyes shifted uncertainly, and

Vlad realized that he hadn't been expecting that question. He must think that Vlad went around making old men into vampires for fun! What a fool!

"You—you can have half of everything that's mine," the magician offered uncertainly.

Vlad looked around. "No, thanks," he said. "I've already got plenty of junk at home. I'm more interested in cash."

"I have a small retirement fund," the magician said.

As he gazed at the old man, Vlad's pupil's dilated until his green eyes looked black. He was very hungry, and unappetizing though the old man seemed, he was definitely available. In fact, he was asking for it. Vlad felt his fangs slip out of their sheaths as he moved closer, the heat of his prey close at hand. The old man smiled as Vlad embraced his bony shoulders. Suddenly the vampire opened his mouth and bit deep into the quivering flesh of the old man's throat. He almost gagged at the smell, but soon blood gushing down his throat sent a surge of warmth through him that lulled his senses to a pleasant numbness. He closed his eyes and dreamed incoherently of rivers of hot blood.

Suddenly he heard a sharp bang behind him. With a jerk, Vlad pulled his teeth free of the old man's neck. Reeling a little, he rose from his victim's body and stared vacantly at the doorway.

"Are you going to take all night?" said Chelsea, bursting in.

Vlad lifted his lip and snarled.

She took a quick step backward. Then she flushed, embarrassed that he had frightened her. Pretending elaborate unconcern, she looked around the room. "Wow, he's got enough junk here, hasn't he?"

Vlad nudged the magician's lifeless body with his toe. "He *had* enough junk, you mean."

"Dead?"

Vlad nodded. "I don't think he had much life in him. He told me he wanted to be a vampire. Why would anybody want to be in that kind of shape for eternity?"

"Stupid," agreed Chelsea. "Any sign of Rina and James?"

"It's Nick that Rina's going to see, not this stupid magician. And when she shows up there, I'll be waiting for her." Vlad licked the blood off his lips. "Let's go. We'd better park the car somewhere else so they won't see it at Nick's and get suspicious."

James saw the two vampires step out of the magician's house into the deepening twilight. As they walked down the path, he half expected them to turn their heads and look up at the woods where he and Rina were hiding. Instead, the vampires reached Chelsea's car unaware that they were being watched. Vlad opened the door and bent to get in. The interior light momentarily illumined his face, and James felt Rina stiffen.

"His face is pink," she whispered. "That means he's been feeding. He must be full of blood."

"The magician!" James gasped. "Do you think Vlad has killed him?"

They watched Chelsea's car pull away from the house. Even before its taillights were out of sight, James grabbed Rina's hand, and they ran down to the house. The back door was unlocked, and they slipped in quietly. They found themselves standing in the room next to the brightly lit table. The table was covered with maps of yellowed parchment with pictures of monsters and dragons as borders. Castles were blacked in here and there on the maps, looking like odd sorts of Monopoly hotels.

"Roger?" Rina called softly. "Roger, are you okay?"

James stepped past the bookcase that served as a divider between the rooms. "No, he's not okay," he said. The magician lay sprawled on the floor, a frozen rictus of horror on his ravaged face. Incongruously, sunglasses lay at his feet. James felt an electric shock of dismay when he saw that at the base of his neck was a yellowish bruise with two white puncture marks. *This could have been me! This is what vampires do—they kill people!*

Rina knelt beside the old man and felt for a pulse. She gasped. "Oh, James, he's dead! He can't help me now!"

Rina's voice jolted James's consciousness back to their immediate problem, and he glanced around anxiously. He was glad the old man had pulled the curtains of the room tightly closed. Vlad and Chelsea must not be far away, and if the curtains had been open, he and Rina would have been visible for miles. "The spell's got to be here somewhere," he said.

"But where?" Rina gazed around the room with dismay. Hundreds of books weighed down the shelves. "Even if we went through all these books, it would take weeks. We don't know what it looks like. And there's no guarantee that the spell is written down. Maybe it's hidden in a recipe file or rolled up in a rug—or maybe he had it memorized, and it died with him!"

James heard the rising note of hysteria in her voice and laid his hand on her shoulder. "Calm down. Let me think." He squeezed his eyes closed, trying to remember everything the magician had said. "Remember when he was talking about the spell and saying he didn't know anything about it? He looked over at this bookshelf." James touched the bookcase that divided the two rooms. "I'll bet the spell is on this shelf. This is where he was looking when he was lying to us."

Rina plucked a worn-looking book from the shelf. "This one doesn't have any dust on top," she observed. Its spine was broken, and the outside cover was in tatters. She laid it on the map table. At once the old book fell open to a page in the middle. Over the ancient print glimmered a long gray hair that had been caught in the pages. "He's been reading it, anyway," she murmured. "That's one of his hairs."

They cast a frightened glance toward the

magician's body, sprawled behind the bookcase. From where they stood, only a shoe was visible.

At the top of the book's page, printed in heavy gothic type, was the heading Transformations. Rina read the spell. "This one is done over a grave." She glanced at James in dismay. "It looks like I have to be buried first!"

A cat screamed outside, making them jump.

"Rina, something's wrong!" James grabbed her hand. "We'd better get out of here!"

Appalled, he heard the hollow sound of footfalls on the front porch stairs. He froze, unsure he could move. Rina ripped two pages out of the book and stuffed them under her waistband. James leaped for the door, pulling Rina out of the house after him. He closed the door behind them gently. The two of them stood stock-still, afraid to move lest the intruder hear their tread. The windows in the back room were not curtained, neither the two windows at the back of the room nor the panes of glass in the back door. If the intruder took it into his head to step into the map room and glance around, they would be clearly visible, huddled together outside the door. Eerily, from his peculiar vantage point, James could see the intruder's reflection on an uncurtained back window of the map room. It was Vlad. The vampire bent and plucked his sunglasses from the floor. Tucking them into a pocket, Vlad sniffed suspiciously at the air, his handsome face contorted. James could hear the vampire's loud snuffling breaths, and he almost stopped breathing himself for fear Vlad would hear him.

Mesmerized, James watched Vlad's reflection in the window glass. Something strange had begun to happen. The vampire's eyes bulged like huge jellybeans until they seemed to swell out of his skull. As James watched, the vampire's head turned glossy, green, and bald. Then the windows of the house rattled suddenly. James clutched Rina's hand and jumped off the back porch. He twisted his ankle, but he could still run. He pulled Rina to the side of the garage and there, standing in the shadow of the building, he froze, unsure which way to go.

"Vlad's changing into a blowfly," Rina gasped, "so he can smell us better and follow us in the dark. Oh, James, where can we hide?"

James's first thought was of Silky, waiting saddled in the nearby pasture. But with Rina, escape on the horse was out. Silky would never let her near.

A buzzing sounded suddenly in the darkness before them. It was so insistent that it seemed to be coming from inside James's head.

"Vlad!" shrieked Rina, clutching James.

James heard the low sound of a car engine and sensed that Chelsea was nearby, but that didn't seem as urgent as getting away from the fly, whose buzz seemed to fill the darkness.

"The neighbors!" he shouted. He jerked Rina along with him. She seemed as weightless as a kite as he ran to the nearest house. She stood beside him shivering as he pounded on the door. The buzzing noise was close behind them now. Suddenly the door opened, and James jumped in, pulling Rina with him. Rina slammed the door shut and leaned shivering against it.

A short, middle-aged man with grizzled black hair quickly turned the key in the lock. Nick Gregory stood staring at them.

"Nick!" Rina cried. "Vlad is after us! You've got to help us!"

A woman and two boys stood wide-eyed in the doorway to the kitchen, the boys clinging to their mother's hands. Nick glanced at his frightened family, then swiftly bent to unlock a heavy chest under a nearby window.

The buzzing had stopped, and James glanced at the door uneasily. Suddenly the door shook with the shock of a hard blow.

"Rina!" Vlad's voice yelled. "Let me in! You belong to me! You'll never escape from me now!"

Rina clung to James tightly as a splintering sound ripped the silence. Nick was holding what looked like an antique pistol and had it pointed at the door.

"Have you forgotten, Nick?" Rina wimpered. "Bullets are no good against vampires!"

Suddenly the door flew open and banged against the wall with a sound like a pistol shot. James was horrified to see that Vlad's mouth was open in a snarl. His eyes looked fathomless and black as he leaped at them.

An explosion sounded. Vlad clutched his hand

to his chest and collapsed. A starburst of red soaked his shirt as he writhed on the floor. There was a sucking sound like water going down a drain, and Vlad shriveled before their eyes. For a split second he was a thin raisin of a young man, and then he dissolved to nothing. Like the skeleton of a leaf, he crumbled, then vanished. Only a heap of clothes remained on the living room floor.

Nick picked up a jeweled earring that winked in the lamplight. James saw that his hand was shaking.

"You killed him!" gasped Rina. "How?"

"Sharpened wooden bullets." Nick glanced at them. "I was afraid he might find me someday. We'd been friends, and he was mad at me for taking off. I knew I'd never have a chance to drive a stake through his heart if he came after me, so I whittled these bullets to fit my old pistol. Not much range, but then, he got pretty close." Nick's faced hardened. "I'm never going back. I've got a family now. I don't want anything to do with vampires." He pointed the gun at Rina.

James stepped in front of her. "We're leaving!"

Nick did not lower the gun as they backed out of the house.

14

A small furry bat released its grip on the window frame outside the Gregorys' living room window and flew desperately for the shelter of the nearby woods. Its mouth was agape, and its ragged fangs showed as it panted in fear. "Chelsea," it gasped as it flapped its wings. A gust of wind buoyed it up and bore it toward the dark woods.

There, safely hidden by the thickness of the trees, it clutched an old lichened oak, hanging shivering from its branch. An owl shrieked in the darkness, and the bat shuddered. Vlad was dead! She had seen him wither and slip into nothingness. Now she was all alone! She had planned to kill Vlad herself, but only after she had James safely in her clutches. It was spooky to have no one she could talk to.

The bat's tiny eyes gleamed. She was desperate to find James now. She was sure that deep inside he still loved her. It was only Rina who had ruined things. If she could get rid of Rina, James would be hers forever.

She preened her fur, trying to collect her thoughts and plan. Where had she parked her car? The shock of what had happened to Vlad had for the moment wiped her consciousness blank, but now she remembered they had left it near the little grocery store in the village. She had figured that a parked car there would be less noticeable and wouldn't prompt a call to the police. She needed to get back to the car and regain human shape. As a bat she could hear absolutely everything, but she was a little shortsighted. For scanning the neighborhood for signs of motion, she needed her own shape back. James and Rina didn't have a car, which meant they couldn't get far. And she wasn't afraid of Rina anymore. The girl had turned soft. Chelsea had seen how she cowered behind James when Vlad broke down the door.

The bat spread her wings and, uttering tiny ultrasonic squeaks to guide her, flew silently into the night. She was very close to catching James. She could feel it in her blood. "Chelsea," said the bat, showing sharp fangs.

Rina shivered as she and James crept silently away. "Do you really think Nick would have shot me?" she whispered.

"Yes," said James. "Look what he did to Vlad." He glanced at Rina quickly. "Are you okay? I guess it must have been a shock to you."

Rina shook her head. "I'm glad he's dead," she said simply. "He could have killed us both."

James straightened his shoulders. Had he really worried that Rina still cared about Vlad? What was the matter with him? He stopped suddenly, glancing ahead at the magician's brightly lit house. "The old guy's body's in there, Rina. What if somebody has called the cops?"

She shot him a frightened glance. "Why would anybody call the cops?"

"They might have heard the gunshot just now. I think we'd better not risk going back inside. We'd have a lot of explaining to do if the police drove up and caught us there."

"We don't have to go in." Rina fished the stiff pages out of her jeans. "I've got the spell right here."

She crept close to the magician's house. Light spilled out the uncurtained windows of the map room in the back of the house, and Rina held a page up close to a window so that the light fell on it. "I'm sure this is the spell," she said. "See where it says Transformations at the top?"

James peered over her shoulder, reading the page rapidly. "I don't know, Rina. All that stuff about burying the vampire? It doesn't sound safe."

"I don't really have to breathe, you know," she said apologetically. "I only breathe out of habit. Being buried is no problem for me."

Rina didn't seem to hear him. She was walking back toward the garage, and James had no choice but to follow her. He had no better plan, he realized. They couldn't go back to Nick Gregory's and ask for advice, that was for sure.

"If the old man did the ceremony over and over again," Rina said slowly, "then it stands to reason he'd have all the stuff he would need right at hand. The coffin, the shovel . . ."

"A flashlight," James added grimly. The moon shone behind heavy clouds, but its light was dim and uncertain.

Rina nodded. "Where do you think he would put stuff like that?"

"Probably in the garage."

The garage door was half open, and they bent their heads and slipped in. Inside it smelled vaguely of oil and mildew, and they found themselves nose-to-nose with a rusty car of ancient vintage. Rina edged past the car, shut the garage door, and flicked on the light. James's eye was drawn at once to the dazzle of three silver shovels leaning in the nearest corner. They looked ceremonial rather than practical, but crumbs of dried clay clung to the spades. They had been used, all right. Pushed up against one wall was a shiny casket.

Rina lifted a heavy flashlight off a dusty shelf over the shovels. "This has got to be it, James! Roger put all the things the spell calls for right here! I'll bet he buried the casket in that vegetable patch!"

James had to admit that the old magician had not struck him as the sort who ate a lot of veggies. He remembered the jars of salsa and cans of beans that had been stacked in the front room. He glanced at Rina. "Okay," he said, "let's get all this stuff out to the garden."

They turned off the light, raised the garage door, then lifted the coffin between them and backed out with it. The old clothesline was silhouetted against the lighted windows and helped James get his bearings. It only took them a minute to make their way to the vegetable patch. When they stepped onto its soft soil, James's sneakers sank a couple of inches into the loam. He knew then that the ground had been dug out and piled back in loosely. Rina had to be right. This was the spot the magician had used for the ceremony.

"I'll get the shovels," he said abruptly. His heart was pounding so hard, he felt dizzy as he walked to the garage. He felt as if he were holding his breath. A magic spell. Rina buried in a coffin. It went against all his instincts.

He heard a soft, uneasy whinnying and glanced over at the nearby pasture. Silky's dark silhouette showed behind the fence. She had heard his voice and was wondering why he didn't take her home to her stable. James felt cold sweat dampening his shirt. Too much depended on him.

He took the two shovels back to the plot and handed one to Rina. He propped the flashlight so that it illumined the center of the vegetable patch. Its slanted beams made the lumps of dirt look mountainous, and it filled the plot with strange shadows. Lit from below, Rina's face took on an unearthly strangeness. They worked silently, tossing spadefuls of soft dirt aside. The soil was loose, and the work went quickly. Soon they had a pit the length of the coffin and just deep enough, James judged, to let him cover it. He wanted no more than three to six inches of dirt on top. If the spell worked, he wouldn't have much time to dig Rina out.

"Okay," said Rina. "I'm getting in."

James took a deep breath as she opened the coffin, exposing the padded white-satin lining within. She scrambled in awkwardly, folding her arms so that she would fit. The coffin had been made for a man over six feet tall, and Rina seemed impossibly small against the white satin.

"Have you got the spell?" she asked.

James looked down at the page unhappily. "Yeah."

"Okay. Then go ahead and bury me." She lowered the top of the coffin with a sharp *clack*.

He pushed the coffin to the edge of the pit and nudged it in, wincing as it thudded down onto the soft dirt. Sweat was beading on his brow, and he knew he had better hurry and do it before his nerve gave out.

He shoveled frantically, heaping the dirt loosely on top of the coffin until the soil was more or less level with that of the surrounding vegetable plot. He reminded himself that Rina didn't need to breathe. She wasn't suffocating under that layer of dirt. But his heart hadn't got the message. It raced in terror.

He swallowed hard and stood on top of the

coffin, his feet sinking into the soft soil. His hand shook as he shone the flashlight on the page of the book. "'All the powers of the West, I call to me,'" he read aloud in an unsteady voice, "'and all the powers and spirits of the East. The winds and spirits of the North, and the warmth and the breezes of the South, I call to me. The forces of the changing season and the spinning stars, I call to me. Everything in its time and its season dies and goes dark. But death blossoms into life and light comes from darkness.'" James could feel a light shining on him, and he was aware of the low rumble of a car engine, but he dared not turn his head to look toward the road. He was determined to finish the spell. "'Bring life to this dark spirit now and return to her that breath that was taken from her body. All of the powers and winds of the earth, listen to me. So be it.'"

James glanced toward the road then and saw that Chelsea's car had been driven right up on the old man's lawn. Its headlights were shining on him, and Chelsea herself was briefly caught in their glare as she ran toward him.

James dropped the shovel and ran. He jerked open the pasture gate and got onto Silky's back with a speed that surprised him. All he could think of was that he had to get in the saddle before she smelled Chelsea and reared up. Silky tossed her head as he guided her out the gate.

"James?" Chelsea stood on the vegetable patch, puzzled that he had disappeared.

James urged the horse out the gate and headed toward the road. As soon as they reached it, he signaled Silky to break into a lope. What if the spell had worked? he thought desperately. Rina would need air. How much time did he have? Two minutes? One?

Chelsea was in her car now. She had spotted him. She must know that Silky wouldn't let her get near on foot, and she was going to try to ram them with the car. James felt headlights on him and urged the horse into a gallop. Her hooves clippity-clopped frantically fast on the pavement. The grocery store was just ahead, but the headlights were dazzlingly bright when he glanced over his shoulder, and he could smell the car's hot engine. Suddenly he desperately pulled on the reins and veered off. The glare of Chelsea's headlights dazzled him as he turned, narrowly dodging the car. He heard the tires squeal on the pavement when she tried to turn, then the noisy impact of metal on metal. James glanced back and saw that she had struck the gas pumps and the car doors had flung open. A loud explosion shook the ground, and Silky bolted. James had to struggle to control her. When they reached the magician's place, he glanced over his shoulder and saw that a column of flame had swallowed Chelsea's car. The Mazda's dark skeleton showed dimly inside the fireball.

Doors of houses were opening, and people were spilling onto the street. James was scarcely conscious that a crowd was gathering. He frantically urged Silky into the yard, and the loud clangor of her hooves fell silent as she trotted onto the lawn. At the vegetable patch, James slid off the horse and groped in the darkness for the shovel. His hands were slick with sweat, and its metal slipped in his hands. His heart felt stuck in his throat as he dug, throwing spadefuls of dirt frantically in all directions. The spade struck wood. James tasted dirt in his mouth as he stooped and, with his gritty fingers, pried the cover open. "Rina!" he cried. Dirt tumbled in on the white satin and onto her motionless figure as he grabbed her arms and pulled her up. Rina gasped and blinked, and James felt tears burn his eyes as he helped her struggle clumsily out of the coffin.

A siren sounded in the distance. James was only dimly conscious of the fireball down the street that burned with the brightness of the sun. He gathered Rina into his arms and drew her close. "Never again," he choked. "Forget those stupid spells. You can just go on being a vampire."

Rina coughed. "I think I got dirt in my throat," she gasped.

James pounded her on the back. "Are you okay?" he asked anxiously.

She nodded. "I thought I was going to die. I needed to breathe so bad. It was so tight and dark in the coffin, and at first it was okay, but then I started getting dizzy, and I guess I blacked out for a second."

"Look at me!" James said urgently. He tilted her

chin up and brushed her hair away from her eyes. "Rina, your eyes are different!"

"Brown?" she asked hopefully. "They used to be brown."

James lifted the flashlight and shone it in her face until she blinked and held her hands in front of her eyes. "Brown!" He laughed. "Ordinary, plain brown."

He let the flashlight fall and grabbed her hands. "The spell worked!"

"It worked?" Rina sounded confused. "Is that why I feel sick to my stomach?"

The curious horse drew close to them and nuzzled James. James laughed. "Let's go home. Come on. I'll boost you up into the saddle."

"No! I'm scared!"

"You want to walk? Look at Silky. It's okay. She knows you're a regular person now." James lifted her into the saddle. Then he climbed up behind her and put his arms around her, grabbing the reins.

"What's that fire!" she cried. "Look!"

James stared. The front of the grocery store was luridly lit by the fire that had swallowed Chelsea's car. "That's the end of Chelsea," he said. "She crashed." James nudged the horse with his knees. "Let's get out of here, Rina. I'd rather not be around when the police show up, okay?"

She nodded.

The neighbors were too focused on the great burst of flame in their midst to notice a single horse making her way in the darkness to the bridle path that went through the woods.

"I can hardly see," said Rina as they rode onto the narrow path.

"It's okay. The horse knows the way. And she's pretty anxious to get home."

Once James's eyes had adjusted to the darkness, he could make out the dim trail and a pale strip of sky overhead. It felt good to be out of sight of the fireball burning at the grocery store below. He didn't like to think of poor Chelsea being caught in that car and reminded himself that she had probably vanished painlessly, just as Vlad had. Vampires had once seemed overwhelmingly powerful to him. But now he realized they were fragile. Not much life was in them after all as they hovered between life and death, and it took only a nudge to send them toppling into nothingness.

Rina, at least, had been saved from the darkness. He sighed happily when he felt her warmth. Against all odds, she was alive.

"I'm cold," complained Rina. "And I feel so stupid and weak."

James laughed. "That's okay. It takes some getting used to, but it's perfectly normal for people to feel stupid." He slipped off his grandfather's jacket and wrapped it around her shoulders. As she struggled to get her arms in the sleeves, he smiled. He lifted her hair out of the collar of the jacket and kissed her neck.

"That tickles," she protested.

"Then turn around and look at me," he teased.

She met his gaze. "This is going to be fun, isn't it?" she said.

He smiled. "I hope so." It was awkward kissing on horseback. Just as James got his lips comfortably pressed to Rina's, Silky bumped, and he bit his lip.

"We need practice," Rina said hopefully.

"Don't worry," said James. As he wrapped his arms around her, he could feel happy laughter bubbling up inside him. "We'll get plenty of it."

THRILLERS

Nobody Scares 'Em Like
R.L. Stine

Seven unforgettable stories guaranteed
to scare you to death. We promise.

BONE MEAL

SEVEN MORE TALES OF TERROR
Edited by A. Finnis

Eunice's parents' garden is
their pride and joy. Too bad their
favorite fertilizer isn't available in
stores. And isn't it strange that
another one of her boyfriends has
mysteriously disappeared....

This and six other terrifying
tales take you on a bone-chilling
ride that you'll never forget.